What the press says about Harlequin Romances…

"…clean, wholesome fiction…always with an upbeat, happy ending."
—*San Francisco Chronicle*

"…a work of art."
—*The Globe & Mail*, Toronto

"Nothing quite like it has happened since *Gone With the Wind*…"
—*Los Angeles Times*

"…among the top ten…"
—*International Herald-Tribune*, Paris

"Women have come to trust these clean, easy-to-read love stories about contemporary people, set in exciting foreign places."
—*Best Sellers*, New York

The Bahamian Pirate

by

JANE CORRIE

Harlequin Books

TORONTO • LONDON • NEW YORK • AMSTERDAM • SYDNEY • WINNIPEG

Original hardcover edition published in 1976
by Mills & Boon Limited

ISBN 0-373-02072-4

Harlequin edition published May 1977

Printed in U.S.A.

CHAPTER ONE

SERENA blinked and stared at the woman by her side, then half shook her head as if to clear the fog that had suddenly descended on her senses.

'Pretend to be your granddaughter?' she said blankly. 'I couldn't possibly! I mean, I know nothing about you. Have you lost touch with your family? If so, perhaps I could make some inquiries for you?' She broke off, still partially recovering from the slightly unusual request from her companion.

Giving the woman another swift side glance, Serena surmised that she was not as old as she had thought at first, but so frail-looking, as if a puff of wind might blow her away. The woman was well wrapped up in a mink coat that Serena knew the price of, as her mother possessed one. Whoever the woman was, she was a lady of means. Serena rather wished she could pass the episode off as an odd whim on the elderly lady's part, but there was a pleading in the faded blue eyes that ruled out this wish. She was not an eccentric, and she was in deadly earnest.

Serena's lovely violet blue eyes met the blue ones squarely. The look of compassion in hers reached through to the older woman. 'Look, I'd like to help you, but I don't see how I can. I'm only on holiday here. In fact, I should have left for New York yesterday,' she explained patiently.

'Couldn't you possibly stay a day or two longer?' pleaded the woman. 'It means so much to me. Oh, dear,' she exclaimed, 'I'm explaining this so very badly. You must think I'm mad. Well, to tell the truth I must have been at the time. I really don't know what possessed me, but Clarissa Simpson would keep on and on about how wonderful her granddaughter was, and wasn't it a shame I had no one, so you see it really wasn't surprising I did such a stupid thing.' She looked at Serena with her head on one side, reminding Serena of an expectant sparrow.

Having a somewhat scatty mother had its advantages at times, Serena thought. She was perfectly able to follow the reasoning. 'So you made a granddaughter up,' she said.

Her companion nodded eagerly. 'You do understand! I knew you would! When I saw you sitting here all alone, you looked—forgive me, dear, for my bluntness—but you looked as if you were trying to come to some decision. As if you needed to be alone to think something over.' She gave Serena a sweet smile. 'I think I would have stopped and spoken to you anyway, but it was the colour of your hair that made me decide to put this outrageous imagined. Her mother had taken Roger at his word and practically bought an entire wardrobe. Gazing bewilderedly at Serena's white face, Mrs Belmont explained that she had only bought what she needed for the holiday, and Roger wouldn't quibble about the price anyway, he was practically family, wasn't he?

On Serena's tight-lipped assertion that she wasn't going to marry Roger, her mother had shrugged her elegant shoulders and said soothingly, 'Nonsense, of course you will, you're quite fond of him really.'

Serena began to see the writing on the wall; slowly but surely she was being drawn into a well-laid trap. It was obvious; Roger knew full well her mother's weakness and had deliberately encouraged her. He'd been extremely clever; he would never mention that account, he was too much of a gentle-man for that—no, he'd known Serena would eventu-ally find out about it, for he knew how strict a watch she had to keep on her mother's spending and soon the pressure would become more than Serena could withstand. Instinctively Serena knew this was only the start; she had been allowed as much rope as he had been prepared to give her, the lasso was now being tightened around her. Her lips straightened; it appeared she had underestimated Roger's deter-mination to marry her. She ought to have known better; men of his calibre did not accept defeat.

Now, after a few days on this beautiful island in

the Bahamas, Serena was no nearer a solution to her problems and couldn't see how she could extricate herself from the subtle bonds that were being woven about her. Feeling a light touch on her arm, she was brought back from her musings.

'You are worried, aren't you, dear?' murmured Mrs Tonetti. 'Forget my stupid suggestion. It was selfish of me to ask it of you. I don't suppose talking over your problem would help, would it? I'm not trying to pry, but I know it sometimes helps. I've often wished in the past I had someone to confide in.'

Serena glanced down at the frail woman by her side. Not only perceptive, but very sweet as well, she thought. She smiled at her, for those few words had helped her to come to one decision at least; she would help Mrs Tonetti if it were at all possible. She would stay the whole week, that would give her three more days on the island. She presumed all she had to do was make an appearance, be introduced as the granddaughter and fade out of the picture.

It could, of course, be tricky; Serena hadn't much experience of duplicity and was not sure she could carry it off, but was game to try. 'I could stay a few days longer,' she said suddenly. 'But I must be on the New York flight on Saturday, or Mother will worry.'

It took a minute or so for Mrs Tonetti to fall in, then she gave Serena a searching look and gasped, 'You mean you'll do it? Pretend to be my granddaughter, I mean?' Impulsively she caught Serena's hand. 'Oh, my dear,' she said, dabbing at her eyes. 'I'll never be able to thank you enough.' Her eyes sparkled as she added, 'Just wait until Clarissa Simpson sets eyes on you!'

'It might not work, you know,' warned Serena. 'I've never done this sort of thing before. Suppose they ask me something and I say the wrong thing? It would be awful if it went wrong, have you thought of that?'

Mrs Tonetti refused to be discouraged. 'I firmly believe in fate, my dear. Why should I suddenly come across you when I'd been so worried about the Centenary celebrations?'

'Centenary celebrations?' echoed Serena.

'That's what it's all about,' replied Mrs Tonetti. 'If I hadn't been so naughty as to fabricate a story about a granddaughter, I wouldn't be in this mess. Never lie, Serena: it just doesn't pay, even though you're sorely tempted—and if Clarissa Simpson wasn't the devil's weapon, I don't know who was! One lie, told in absolute frustration, can completely snowball as this one did. She won't let me forget it. Always mentions my granddaughter and how I must miss her, and wasn't it strange she never came to see me.' She sighed. 'I even had an old friend in England post out letters now and again to keep the deception up. In this part of the world. you know, there's not much goes on that isn't noticed.'

Serena tried to compose herself, but the ironies of the situation were too much for her and she broke out into a deep chuckle. Mrs Tonetti gave her a surprised look. 'Sorry,' smiled Serena, 'but having just agreed to become your accomplice I find the advice a little untimely!'

Mrs Tonetti tried to look stern but failed, and gave a little chuckle herself. 'Well, perhaps what I should have said was take a lesson from what happened to me,' she said.

'You were telling me about the Centenary celebrations,' Serena reminded her.

'Oh, yes,' answered Mrs Tonetti. 'It's quite a big occasion, you know. In fact, quite a lot of visitors will turn up for it. We have one or two occasions during the year, but this one is special. The whole island has a holiday, they'll even re-enact the landing all those years ago of the pirates who took the island by storm. Jordan's ancestors, you know.'

'Er ... Jordan?' queried Serena, once again beginning to feel lost.

'Jordan Kerr, dear, the owner of the island. You'll meet him, of course. Such a sweet man, he'll be very pleased to meet you, he's asked after you often, purely for kindness' sake, I assure you. I hated deceiving him, you know, he's been so thoughtful and kind to me since I came here to live, but he's like that, takes everyone's welfare on his shoulders, and he's such a busy man too.' She gave Serena a bright-eyed look. 'Not everyone can settle here, you know. He vets them first.' She gave a slight shiver and gathered her coat around her.

'Ought you to be out now that it's getting chilly?' Serena asked.

'Not really, I know. The doctor did warn me ...' Mrs Tonetti broke off suddenly. 'Well, you know what it is when you get old. They always want to coddle you, but it would be rather foolish to catch a chill just when life starts getting exciting.'

Serena was not feeling quite so happy about the situation. Quite a lot of people, it seemed, had heard about the mythical granddaughter. This Jordan Kerr, for instance: well, it depended what sort of a man he was. If he really was as kind as Mrs Tonetti said he was, it might perhaps be wise to let him in on the deception, for if things went wrong Mrs Tonetti could depend on him to smooth things over. She put this to her companion.

'My dear, I couldn't possibly! You don't understand. I couldn't bear it if he knew I was such a ... wicked liar!'

She spoke with such vehemence and got so upset about it, Serena did not press the point. In any case, Mrs Tonetti seemed anxious to drop the subject.

'Where are you staying?' she asked Serena quickly.

'The Royal,' Serena replied.

'A wise choice,' Mrs Tonetti remarked. 'Not that

the other two are bad, but the Royal is considered the best. However, I do not intend to put you to the expense of spending two more days there, their rates are not all that cheap. We'll collect your luggage, and you must come and stay with me, it would look odd if you didn't.'

Having agreed to help, Serena had now burnt her boats. Mrs Tonetti was right, it would look odd if she continued to reside at the hotel. She was glad she had spent the last two days avoiding contact with other residents; spending her time taking long solitary walks among the hills framing the old harbour, Serena had wanted no distractions, for she had a lot on her mind.

As they slowly descended the slight incline down to the hotel grounds, it occurred to Serena that it was a pity she had not inherited her mother's penchant for bizarre situations. Had she been thus approached she would have been in the seventh heaven and plunged into the role with uninhibited enthusiasm —what was more, she would carry it off to perfection. Mrs Belmont did not believe in half-measures!

As they neared the hotel, Serena was grateful they did not have much further to go. Her companion seemed to tire easily, and she wondered how they were going to get to wherever it was that Mrs Tonetti lived. Serena could not possibly carry her three cases, and Mrs Tonetti obviously could not help. She knew there was a shortage of taxis on the island as she had had to wait at the small air terminal for one on her arrival, and she had heard tourists at the hotel complaining about the shortage. Serena remarked on this to Mrs Tonetti.

'We're only a small island, you know, dear,' answered Mrs Tonetti. 'I don't think there's more than half a dozen all told, and at this time of day they'd be pretty busy with fares wanting to visit the night clubs. Even so, residents are given precedence.'

When they arrived at the hotel Mrs Tonetti proved her case, as within ten minutes of Serena packing, a private car stood waiting outside the hotel.

Serena's cases were carried out of the hotel and put in the boot of the car by a tall West Indian wearing the uniform of the hotel, and as they got in the car, Mrs Tonetti met Serena's raised brows with a smile. 'Residents, dear—as I told you, we're very well looked after. Straight home, Charles,' she ordered as the man settled himself behind the wheel.

Mrs Tonetti's residence lay beyond the island's small township. Serena could not see much once they had left the twinkling lights of the main street behind. The journey took only ten minutes or so. The lights were on in the porch of the sprawling chalet-type dwelling they drew up in front of. Charles, as Mrs Tonetti had addressed him, carried the cases into the hall and with a grin that spread from ear to

17

ear, wished them goodnight before returning to the hotel.

'Molly?' called Mrs Tonetti as she led the way through the hall. 'Come and see who I've got with me.' In an undertone she murmured to Serena, 'My housekeeper.'

A few seconds later a stout Negress in a sedate green overall waddled towards them, her white teeth gleaming in a welcoming smile that seemed to come so naturally to these natives of the islands.

'Serena, meet Molly. My absolute treasure, cook, housekeeper, and general dogsbody, eh, Molly?' said Mrs Tonetti, smiling encouragingly at her. 'This, Molly, is Serena, my granddaughter. How's that for a surprise?'

Molly's welcoming smile broadened, she held out a large brown hand and took Serena's in hers. 'Sure am pleased you come, missy. Now Missus okay, eh?' She beamed at her employer.

Mrs Tonetti nodded slowly, her smile a little tremulous this time. For a second Serena felt a brush of sadness in that smile, then as quickly as she had become aware of it, it had gone. Mrs Tonetti moved into a room leading off the hall, drawing Serena with her. 'I'm sure Serena would like a pot of tea while we wait for dinner,' she called to Molly before she settled Serena into a comfortable cane-backed chair.

Once seated herself, she let out a sigh of pure relief and Serena noted how tired she was, and again wondered how old she was. Her beautifully waved white hair framed her delicate almost ivory features. High cheekbones, now with the skin stretched tightly over them, gave a hint of the beauty she must once have been. The blue eyes, now faded, would in her youth, have been devastating. Serena sighed inwardly; it must be terrible to be completely alone, she thought.

Mrs Tonetti rested her head back on her chair and gave Serena a sweet smile. 'Now we can talk,' she said conspiratorially.

'Ought you to have given Molly my real name?' queried Serena. 'What name did you give your granddaughter?'

'Oh, don't worry about that,' answered Mrs Tonetti quickly. 'It's Lisa, as a matter of fact, but I thought it might complicate things if you had to remember to answer to the name. You see, my dear, I've not only manufactured a relation, but a career for her as well. It was the only thing I could think of to give you some excuse for not coming to see me.' She gave Serena another of her delightful smiles accompanied by a half apologetic look. 'It's rather a glamorous career, too.'

Serena blinked and hoped it wasn't anything in the film line, for if she were asked any questions about the movie world she would be stumped for a start.

'You're a model, dear,' explained Mrs Tonetti. 'Not as yet top class, but with a little luck and hard work, you should make the top grade.'

'Thank you,' answered Serena solemnly, her eyes brimming with mischief. 'I shall endeavour to do my best.'

Her companion chuckled. 'So convenient, isn't it? Your name is so perfect for the role. Your height, too!' She studied Serena with her head on one side. 'Not only that, but your clothes, my dear. If you don't mind my saying so, you do rather look as if you have already made the grade. That's a Balmain suit unless I'm very much mistaken.'

Serena nodded, and was about to ask whether she had mentioned where she was supposed to be working, when the door opened after a soft tap and Molly appeared with a tray of tea things. When she left, Serena asked her question.

'Oh, London, dear. At least you're stationed there. You do travel back and forth on the Continent for the fashion shows.'

As she accepted a cup of tea, Serena thought there should be no difficulty there. She knew at least four fashion houses in London, and one in Paris. It would be easy to mention one of them and she had the added good fortune to be quite friendly with one top flight model. So far, so good—there was just one little problem. 'Are my parents alive?' she asked, smiling inwardly at the thought of her mother's indignant reaction to the question had she been privileged to hear it.

Sipping her tea slowly, Mrs Tonetti swallowed and shook her head. 'No, dear. There's only you and I, so don't worry about that side of things, it was all explained away.'

'What am I to call you? I'm afraid I don't remember my own grandparents,' Serena said.

Mrs Tonetti appeared to give this question some thought. 'I never did like being called "Gran", I think I would prefer "Nan"—what do you think?'

Serena heartily agreed; she had no inclination towards the name Gran. Somehow it would seem impertinent. 'When is the Centenary?' she asked.

'Thursday,' replied Mrs Tonetti, a note of satisfaction in her voice. 'There's a Centenary Eve Ball at Jordan's home tomorrow evening,' she gave Serena a hesitant glance. 'I'd rather like to take you there. I think it would be a good place for you to make your first appearance. Not the sort of place where an inquisition can be held, if you see what I mean. There'll be introductions, of course, and you'll obviously be asked to dance,' she broke off chuckling. 'In fact, my dear, I shall be very surprised if you aren't stampeded—and that,' she said a little maliciously, 'will keep you out of Clarissa Simpson's prying eyes. She'll be so frustrated! I just can't wait to present you to her.'

'What exactly happens on Thursday?' queried Serena.

'Well, as I've said, they do this landing thing, all dressed up as pirates. I don't know whether Jordan will take part on the day itself, or not. They had a rehearsal the other day, and you should have been here, my dear, it was wonderful—Jordan dressed as his forebears, with a scarf around his forehead and in the dress of the day. He was the image of a portrait in his library of the first Jordan Kerr who took the island all those years ago.' She gave a sigh. 'You know, those must have been exciting times, sometimes I rather wish I'd been part of them.'

Serena shivered, not because of any change of temperature in the room, which was pleasantly warm, but she quite suddenly had a vision of a bunch of marauding pirates wading ashore, knives in their mouths and cutlasses swinging. Heaven help anyone who got in their way! She, for one, was thankful those days were over.

'And then,' went on Mrs Tonetti, 'we have a carnival parade through the town and that takes most of the morning. In the afternoon, there's canoe racing and a barbecue on the shore. Later, another dance at Jordan's place. It's a very hectic time, and of course, I shall keep you with me the whole time, so you won't have to worry about saying the wrong thing. You did say you had to leave on Saturday, didn't you, dear?'

Serena nodded. 'Don't you think it would be a better idea if I were to take off on Friday instead of Saturday?' she asked.

Mrs Tonetti looked woebegone. 'Oh, do stay another day, dear. You won't have to meet anyone, I shall say you're going on Saturday and that I intend to have you to myself for that one day. Not even Clarissa Simpson can argue with that!' She gave Serena a hopeful look. 'I do so enjoy having company. I really don't get much these days, I have a stupid complaint that prevents me doing too much in the social line. Don't look so alarmed, my dear,' she added hastily, 'what else can you expect at my age? Will you stay until you really have to go?'

Serena would have liked to have gone on Friday, but she had no defence against those pleading blue eyes. Smiling wryly, she gave in. 'Saturday, then,' she said.

CHAPTER TWO

AFTER a delicious meal of chicken cooked in a rich wine and garnished with button mushrooms, tiny shallots and herb sauce, followed by a fresh cream gateau, Serena and her hostess relaxed in the spacious beautifully furnished lounge.

Declining the offer of a liqueur, Serena protested, 'Really, I've had ample. I hate to think what would happen to my figure should I stay here for long. Do you always have such mouthwatering dishes?'

Mrs Tonetti smiled. 'No, my dear, Molly never gets the chance to show off with just me. I usually exist on some kind of light diet. I expect you noticed the tiny portion she allotted me, as a sort of a treat, you know. I'm afraid I haven't much of an appetite these days. You'd never believe some of the dishes she puts before me were some form of fish or chicken, she's a genius at disguise; not only that, they taste delicious as well.'

Silence fell between them while they sipped their coffee. Serena's thoughts were busy with the forth-coming events; would it all be as easy as her extra-ordinary but beguiling companion thought it would be? She could well understand the loneliness and frustration that had made Mrs Tonetti invent a relation. Going back to her childhood days, Serena could remember how often she was tempted to do the same thing at her boarding school, but her invention would have been a brother or sister. How often had she listened to her friends and their tales of the doings of their family; of Patsy Johnson's irresponsible brothers and the tangles they got into.

As an only child, Serena had felt left out of things. She sighed; yes, she could see the old lady's point of view. This Clarissa Simpson must be an insufferable person to have driven a lonely, harmless woman to such lengths of deception. Thinking back to their previous conversation, Serena remembered something that had puzzled her; what had Mrs Tonetti said about not liking being called 'Gran'? Almost, mused Serena, as if she had once been addressed as such. Had the fantasy taken such a hold of her that in her mind the granddaughter really did exist?

A wave of compassion touched her, and Serena was determined to do all she could to help Mrs Tonetti. For a short space of time it would take her mind off her own troubles. Time enough to face up to them when she joined her mother and Roger in New York on Saturday.

Glancing across at Mrs Tonetti, Serena found her making an effort to keep awake, but her lids were gradually drooping; she must have missed her afternoon siesta, Serena thought.

'Would you like to go to bed?' Serena asked her gently. 'I've some unpacking to do and would welcome an early night myself.'

Mrs Tonetti made another effort to rouse herself. 'I shouldn't be surprised if Molly hasn't already unpacked for you, dear,' she murmured drowsily. 'But I must agree it's time I rested, especially if I mean to do a little socialising in the next few days.' She smiled at Serena. 'So if you'll excuse me, I shall go to bed.'

On reaching the door, she turned and gave Serena another smile. 'Molly would have put you in the best guest room; she'll take you there when you're ready.' She hesitated for a second, then added softly, 'You can't imagine how grateful I am to you, my dear. We'll have a nice long chat in the morning.'

While Serena waited for Molly to collect the coffee tray she glanced through some magazines lying on a side table. They were mostly American, similar to the more exclusive journals printed in England. There were articles on the doings of the high society, gossip columns, and the usual speculation on who would eventually marry whom. Serena's eye caught a paragraph that mentioned a name she had heard recently—Jordan Kerr. Her brows rose as she read the news snip.

'Jordan Kerr, wealthy owner of Blue Island in

the Bahamas (incidentally, reported in our last issue as one of the six most eligible bachelors in the world!), was spotted lunching with the delectable Miss Myrna Simpson at Kilroy's on Friday. Will another diehard soon bite the dust?'

No photograph accompanied the news item, and Serena was a little disappointed, for she would have liked to have seen what Jordan Kerr looked like. She was also a little surprised to find the man Mrs Tonetti talked of in such warm tones coming under the category of one of the world's most eligible bachelors; not that that automatically made him a playboy, but it somehow did not gell with the description Mrs Tonetti had given of him. A little smile played round Serena's mouth as she thought of Mrs Tonetti's reaction to that paragraph. Myrna Simpson, she mused, would be Clarissa Simpson's granddaughter, the one who kept all the bachelors on their toes.

A short while later Molly appeared. 'Missus said you'd like to go to your room, Miss Serena,' she said shyly.

Serena smiled at her. 'Yes, please, Molly, if you would show me the room you've put me in.'

The room Molly took her to could have been no other than the best guest room, as Mrs Tonetti had surmised it would be, and was certainly extra special. It was purely feminine; the main colour theme was peach and a delicate pastel blue. Peach linen on the bed and a beautiful embroidered bed-spread of peach and blue blossoms echoed the delicate hues of the pastel walls and the blue velvet curtaining. There was an ornate dressing table with gold-framed mirrors and an exquisite brush set, the backs of which were decorated with paintings of peach blossom on a blue background; Serena did not have to examine them to know they were antique and highly valuable.

Serena's gaze slid round the room, at the thick carpet, a darker blue than the curtains, the chairs with dainty spindled legs, another collector's item, and a gorgeous full-length mirror framed in an al-cove next to the inbuilt wardrobe that ran the length of the room. The bedside lamp next caught her attention, and she moved to the cabinet beside the bed to have a closer look at it, and caught her breath. It was enchanting; a nymph with deli-cately sculptured limbs held a torch above her head in what could only be described as a triumphant pose. Serena was not sure, but rather suspected the metal was just what it appeared to be, gold. She wondered whether Mrs Tonetti had any idea she was living in a collector's paradise. It was just as well, Serena thought, that Jordan Kerr vetted all newcomers to the island, for had Mrs Tonetti elec-ted to live elsewhere, her life would have been one long fight against the intrusion of collectors or their agents.

Undressing, Serena smiled as she noted that Molly had even gone to the extent of laying out her nightdress and negligée. She was certainly receiving V.I.P. treatment!

After her bath, Serena returned to the bedroom and stood before the dressing table wondering where Molly could have put her toilet case. Having apparently packed hers away, it was obvious she expected Serena to use the beautiful set laid out on the dressing table, but Serena felt this would be an encroachment and looked for her own, eventually finding the case in the top drawer of the dressing table. As she took it out, a photograph caught her eye and she looked closer at it.

It was of a girl standing against a background of rocks. Whoever had taken the photograph had not been an expert; the girl was shading her eyes against the glare of the sun and her features were partly in shadow. She was tall, with long dark hair, and judging by the style of the dress she wore, the snap was probably taken about five years ago. Serena could well remember wearing a similar style when she was eighteen.

There was a name scrawled at the bottom of the snap, and Serena bent closer to read it and frowned when she made out the name 'Lisa'. Closing the drawer, she sat for a few minutes staring at her reflection in the mirror, then started brushing her hair. Was that where Mrs Tonetti had got the name from? Was she a daughter of a friend? Serena recalled her words about not liking being called Gran, then she shrugged. Mrs Tonetti could have got that snap from anywhere, sent perhaps from England; the background rather suggested England than a sub-tropical island in the Bahamas. She would have to have something to show folk in order to prove the existence of the fabricated granddaughter.

Having seen the photograph Serena could now understand why she had caught Mrs Tonetti's attention. The girl in the photograph might well have been herself; there was a curious likeness there, and they were about the same height. The fact that the features were obscured was a point in Mrs Tonetti's favour, and Serena half-smiled; no wonder she had thought Serena the answer to her problem!

A tiny frown creased her forehead. Mrs Tonetti must have often regretted the mad impulse that had placed her in this position. Serena wasn't sure she was helping things either; to appear, then disappear, would surely complicate matters further. She gave this some thought, then brightened. She could send her a letter now and then, in fact, she decided, smiling at her reflection, she would adopt Mrs Tonetti as her official grandmother! She couldn't think of a nicer person to fill the role! On these thoughts Serena climbed into bed and was soon fast asleep.

Mrs Tonetti was not an early riser, and Serena breakfasted alone on the patio at the back of the chalet. She was quite content to laze in the warm sunshine and gaze at the panorama spread out before her. The gardens front and back were quite large, but beautifully kept, from what Serena could see of them. She decided to ask permission later to explore them.

Her eyes dwelt on the splashes of colour; pinks, blues, bright reds and brilliant whites all proclaimed a gardener's paradise. She heard the calls of birds and the strident screech of the brightly coloured parakeets as they flew by intent on their search for food. As the perfume of the flowers floated towards her, Serena took a deep breath. How heavenly, she thought, to be able to call a place like this your own. Her worries seemed to recede in this peaceful setting. It was as well she was leaving on Saturday, she thought, for she had a feeling that a longer stay would make it impossible for her to leave. She sighed wearily. It was no use indulging in wishful thinking; she had to face the future. There was her mother to consider.

'You're back to your problems, aren't you, Serena?'

Serena gave a small start and turned to give a rueful smile to Mrs Tonetti.

'Are you sure you wouldn't like to talk about them? I'd like to help, if I can. If you'd let me, that is ...' Mrs Tonetti ended a little hesitantly, not wanting to intrude on Serena's private life unless given permission.

'I don't see why I should burden you with my problems,' Serena said gently. 'To be honest, I'm not sure there is an answer, apart from the one I'm trying to avoid.'

Not quite knowing how it happened, she found herself telling the whole story. In a way it was a relief to talk about it. There was no one else she could confide in. All her friends were friends of her mother and Roger, and if asked would say she was foolish to turn Roger down. Jean Woodson, for instance, who adored Roger and would marry him tomorrow were she but given the chance, would think Serena mad for even considering refusing him.

Mrs Tonetti listened attentively, only interrupting once to ask how old Roger was, and was silent for a while after Serena had finished explaining the position.

'Well, one thing is certain, dear,' she said gently. 'You're not to even consider marriage unless you love the man. As for your mother, I know it sounds callous, but isn't it about time she learnt to stand on her own two feet? The more you shield her from her own stupidity the longer she'll take to realise her responsibilities. You can't be expected to go on protecting her from the realities of life.'

Serena sighed. 'Oh, I know you're right, but if

you only knew Mother! She hasn't ever had to fend for herself. She'd be game to try, you know, but she wouldn't have a clue. Father managed everything— and he did rather spoil her. He spoilt me, too, come to that.' There were tears in her eyes as she said this and it took a second or two to compose herself before going on, 'I feel awful about it, but I can't help hoping she could meet someone like him again. I know it's what he'd want, too. She isn't short of admirers, she's still quite lovely, and there's a good possibility that she might meet someone on this cruise Roger's got lined up. I do know he's asked several of his New York business acquaintances to join us. He's pretty astute, you know, and I wouldn't mind betting he's already lined up a few presentable types who might fit the bill.'

Serena looked away and concentrated her gaze on a lovely purple blossom entwined on a trellis running the length of the low patio wall. 'I was so grateful to him,' she went on tonelessly. 'But when I found out what he was up to, encouraging Mother to splash out like that, I was furious with him—still am, as a matter of fact. He knows how much I hate being in debt to anyone,' she sighed. 'He's often told me I'm too independent, but someone in the family has to watch points if we're to keep our heads above water.'

'And your mother is in New York now, is she?' Mrs Tonetti asked.

Serena nodded. 'Yes, I told her to go on ahead. She's all right on her own, we've several friends there and they'll look after her until I join her on Saturday. Roger will be free by then, too. The cruise starts the following Monday—that reminds me, I ought to cable her and tell her I won't be joining her until the weekend. She was expecting me tomorrow.'

'Do so right away, then,' urged Mrs Tonetti. 'Use the phone.'

After Serena had made the call she rejoined her hostess on the patio, remarking cheerfully, 'You're right, it is a small island! Whoever took the cable was consumed with curiosity about me. She knew where I was speaking from and short of actually asking me who I was and why I was here, she tried everything else in the book! I didn't give my surname, just signed the cable Serena.'

Mrs Tonetti chuckled and all but clapped her hands. 'That would have been Beryl Johnson, I'm sure. By this evening it will have got round the whole island that I have a visitor named Serena. I wonder if they'll guess who you are?'

'Oh, dear, does that mean you'll have floods of visitors tomorrow?' Serena queried worriedly.

Mrs Tonetti chuckled again. 'No, dear, it's the ball tomorrow evening, remember? They'll know better than to expect me to entertain if I intend to go, and I shall let it be known that I will be present.'

'Oh, I see,' said Serena, not really seeing at all.

Nevertheless, she was slightly relieved, wanting to put off the actual moment of duplicity as long as possible.

'I've been thinking,' Mrs Tonetti remarked consideringly. 'When you were sending off the cable, it occurred to me that your best course would be to invent another young man. This Roger of yours would have to give up the pursuit if you found someone else, wouldn't he? You could even make that your excuse for not joining them until Saturday,' she added brightly.

Serena found herself chuckling. 'You're incorrigible,' she scolded gently. 'Soon I'll be as bad as you are.' Then she looked serious and slowly shook her head. 'It wouldn't work, I'm afraid. You don't know Roger. I'd not only have to present the mythical young man but show him an engagement ring to boot! The only reason I've been left in peace for a few days is because he doesn't know which island I'm staying on. When Mother gets that cable I expect to hear from him directly. If it weren't for the conference he'd be here on the next plane.'

Mrs Tonetti looked somewhat despondent, then brightened. 'Well, there's time enough yet, dear. We've several nice young men on the island and you just might meet the right one at the ball. I'm a firm believer in fate, as I believe I did tell you, and I'm sure it wasn't just chance that you picked this island to try and find a solution to your problems.'

Serena wished she could echo this sentiment, but was rather of the opinion that it had been sheer chance she had chosen the island—that, and the plain simple fact that she had liked the name of the island, for blue was her favourite colour, and she really didn't think fate had much to do with it at all.

Mrs Tonetti retired after lunch, leaving Serena free to explore the gardens, kept in such immaculate order by Thomas, Molly's brother. She told Serena, 'He comes every day for a few hours, and he should be around somewhere, so do ask him anything you want to know. He's immensely proud of his work and rightly so.'

As she strolled through the grounds Serena looked back at the chalet, admiring the way the building sat on its elevated position overlooking one of the many small bays that surrounded this island paradise. It was quite a large establishment and she did wonder why Mrs Tonetti had chosen it. A cottage or a smaller bungalow would have been ample for her wants, she thought, particularly as she had decided to retire there.

The gardens sloped gently down a terraced incline and Serena found Thomas, or to be more precise, Thomas found her admiring some huge purple convolvulus. The blooms were at least three inches in diameter and absolutely begged for attention. Serena was able to recognise a lot of the flowers and the variety surprised her. With delight she spotted species of honeysuckle, its sweet perfume drifted towards her as she stood admiring a mass of brilliant orange nasturtiums thinking with wonder of their English counterparts that seemed to be almost dull in comparison, a poor relation indeed to these exotic blooms. Such was the case of each species she recognised, the flowers larger, the colour intensified to an almost translucent beauty.

One plant evaded her and she asked Thomas its name. It had large fleshy leaves and pendulous flowers of a green and purple colour and grew in profusion, appearing every now and again in between the riot of flowers and seemed to act as a foil for their brilliance. 'What is that plant, Thomas?' she asked.

Thomas, unlike his sister, was tall and thin, and a little shy, but eager to be helpful. He gave Serena a grin that showed white even teeth. 'Don't rightly know, missy, but we call them Poppers.'

Serena frowned. 'What an odd name,' she commented. 'Must be an abbreviation of the botanical name.'

Thomas grinned again and picked up his spade. 'See, missy,' he said, and selected a large bud of the plant on the point of opening, and to Serena's surprise gave it a sharp tap with the spade. The next moment there was a loud crack sounding like a mild explosion in the sultry stillness of the garden.

'Good gracious!' commented Serena. 'It ought to be called "crackers"!'

Thomas accompanied her on the rest of the tour of the gardens. The rear garden was, if anything, more beautifully laid out than the front. Terraces with frangipani-entwined arches covered the walks. Here shrubs were more in evidence, all in full flower and forming partitions from one section of the garden to another.

It was at the end of the grounds that they came across the part of the garden that Serena fell in love with. The lawns had been replaced by a small paved courtyard, and a rose-like flower grew in profusion on trellises surrounding the area. In the middle of the courtyard stood a lovely statue of a nymph holding an urn on one graceful shoulder. Serena stood entranced. There was peace in this corner of the garden and she sensed it was somehow special. The layout inevitably reminded her of Italian gardens and their love of courtyards and neatness combined with beauty. She felt she knew now why Mrs Tonetti had chosen this particular place to retire to. She sighed; it made her feel a little sad, for it was obvious that the old lady had loved her husband very much.

Her thoughts were communicated to Thomas. 'Mr Tonetti, he came here often,' he said, and indicated a small covered archway with seating accommodation for two. 'Now, only Missus come.'

Serena looked at Thomas in surprise. 'Did you

know Mr Tonetti, Thomas?'

Thomas nodded. 'He and Missus come every year for holiday. Always have this place. Boss said keep it for Mrs Tonetti.'

She frowned. Boss? did he mean Mr Tonetti?

Thomas's next words answered her unspoken question. 'Plenty like to get this place. Mrs Simpson always on at Boss, wants to buy it, but Boss likes Mrs Tonetti, he won't sell.'

Things were getting a little clearer to Serena now. No wonder Mrs Tonetti didn't like Mrs Simpson, and vice versa! Mrs Simpson was obviously put out because this boss, whoever he was, preferred to have Mrs Tonetti as a paying guest rather than receive hard cash at what Serena surmised would be a fabulous figure. Properties in this part of the world could rise to almost astronomical heights.

CHAPTER THREE

WEDNESDAY evening and Serena's debut as Mrs Tonetti's granddaughter came all too soon for her. She had enjoyed two days of idyllic peace and cosy chats with her charming hostess, to whom Serena was growing very attached.

Now the time had come for her to fulfill her promise, and as she dressed for the ball she found herself wondering how she had ever let herself be talked into the masquerade in the first place. It was too late now to back out and she would have hated herself for trying, but she couldn't help wishing Mrs Tonetti would decide to call the whole thing off.

Upbraiding herself for her cowardice, Serena gave her attention to the dress she would wear and eventually chose the deceptively simple velvet one of midnight blue with long full sleeves buttoning at the wrists. The dress clung to her slender figure and the neck not too low, dipped into a sedate V which emphasised the creamy whiteness of her neck. Her only ornament was a long gold filigree chain necklet of flowers and leaves entwined. This had been her father's gift on her twenty-first birthday and was her favourite piece of jewellery.

Before joining Mrs Tonetti, Serena gave herself

one last critical inspection; her glance passed down the dress to the gold sandals on her feet, she then stood back from the mirror to get a glimpse of the overall effect and frowned as an odd sensation swept over her. She didn't feel at all real and her reflection solemnly staring back at her accentuated this feeling. She had left her hair long and parted in the middle, and it fell in a dark cloud on her shoulders to frame her pale features. Her eyes looked enormous and she wondered whether she ought to have chosen a slightly darker eye-shadow instead of the greenish-blue one that appeared to highlight her eyes so much. She wasn't sure whether it was the dress that gave her such a wraithlike appearance, almost, she mused, as if she had stepped out of medieval times, making her feel there should have been a knight in attendance somewhere.

She grimaced at her reflection. Bizarre situations brought bizarre thoughts, didn't they? and shrugged impatiently, she was just being fanciful. Taking a deep breath she collected her stole and evening bag. It was all in keeping with her role; models were supposed to stand out in a crowd. These thoughts brought her no comfort, and as she walked towards the lounge to join Mrs Tonetti, the first pangs of nervousness assailed her and her fingers gripped her evening bag more firmly. She must remember to give Mrs Simpson a wide berth. From all she had heard of that lady she was the most formidable obstacle she was likely to meet.

Mrs Tonetti sat quietly awaiting her and did not at first see Serena as she entered the room. Serena saw she was lost in thought and a hope that she might be considering changing her mind about going through with the deception sprang into life. Her plain black silk dress, relieved only by a single string of pearls, drew added attention to her fragility and Serena was on the point of asking her whether it might not be a good idea to forgo the ball, when Mrs Tonetti became aware of her presence and gave a gasp of delight. 'Oh, my dear,' she said softly. 'Paris —Pierre, it couldn't be anyone else!'

Serena's brows rose. For an old lady she certainly knew about fashion! She nodded. 'Yes, but how ...' she began.

Mrs Tonetti smiled. 'We lived in Paris for a while not long after we were married,' she explained. 'Pierre was a special friend of ours, he was only just beginning in those days, but I'd know his creations anywhere. You know,' she added wistfully, 'I only wish he could see you in that gown. He must have had you in mind when he created it.'

The sound of a car drawing up in front of the house put an end to the conversation, and to any hope Serena was secretly nursing about a cancellation. Mrs Tonetti picked up her wrap and Serena placed it over her shoulders for her. 'Thank you, my dear,' she smiled, and sniffed appreciatively. 'I'm a little behind with the perfumes,' she said with twinkling eyes. 'But I like it, whatever it is. Now, are you ready for the fray?' she asked brightly as they moved towards the door.

Serena's stomach started churning again, but she put a brave face on it and managed to smile back at her. 'I only hope I don't let you down,' she replied, trying to sound airy about it.

Mrs Tonetti patted her arm. 'Of course you won't, and if anything does go wrong, and I really don't see how it could, it will be entirely my own fault. I ought to have known better.' She gave Serena a wicked look and added conspiratorially, 'Isn't it exciting? I wouldn't have missed it for worlds!'

As they left the chalet Serena couldn't help wishing once again that she had more of her mother's character in her, not to mention courage!

The car waiting to convey them to their destination was an opulent Rolls, and not an early model either, in fact the very latest on the market, Serena suspected, but surely a little unusual to be used as a taxi service she thought.

'Jordan's, dear,' Mrs Tonetti supplied in answer to Serena's unspoken query. 'So kind of him, isn't it?'

A thin wiry man detached himself from the driving seat and walked towards them.

'Good evening, Jake,' greeted Mrs Tonetti. 'This is my granddaughter, Serena.' She turned to Serena.

'Jake is Jordan's jack-of-all-trades, almost as useful as my Molly, eh, Jake?'

Serena caught the flash of white teeth at this gentle raillery, but could see little else of the man as he stood in the shadows. He spoke in a soft sing-song voice and she hazarded a guess that he was probably Polynesian. 'Pleased to meet you, Miss Serena.'

During the short ride, Mrs Tonetti inquired soli-citously after Jake's wife and family, and all, it appeared, were doing well. During this exchange Serena was able to follow her own thoughts, and she thought of Jordan Kerr. The more she heard about him, the more she warmed to the man. He must be extremely busy, but he found time to see to the wel-fare of an old lady—not that Mrs Tonetti was just any old lady, she was a sweetie, but nevertheless not many in his position would bother. Suddenly she was sure that if anything did go wrong with the pro-posed scheme she had only to tell the truth and he would see that Mrs Tonetti received no backlash. On these thoughts Serena's fears slipped away from her. She could now go on to join her mother and Roger in New York with the comforting knowledge that all would be well. As the car swept down a long bordered drive and drew up in front of an imposing mansion, she found herself actually looking forward to the evening's entertainment.

The strains of dance music drifted towards them

as they mounted the stone steps to the entrance of the house. Serena looked about her with interest. Two stone pillars supported the ground entrance porch and lighting from the open windows lime-lighted the bordering flowering shrubs flanking the entrance. Bougainvillaea in brilliant colours crept round the stone verandah and two stone nymphs holding urns of yet more exotic blossoms stood either side of the great studded doors of the house, now thrown open to welcome guests. For a moment Serena stood inhaling the perfume-laden air, then noting the fact that they were alone with no other guests either arriving or in the immediate vicinity, she asked, 'Are we very late?'

Taking her arm and leading her into the house, Mrs Tonetti replied, 'A little late, yes, dear.'

A young West Indian girl in a brightly coloured sarong drifted towards them one slender arm extended to take their stoles. 'Ah, May,' greeted Mrs Tonetti smilingly. 'We shall be going early, dear, so leave them somewhere handy, won't you?'

The special smile the girl gave in answer proved once again to Serena that Mrs Tonetti was not only respected but well liked by the islanders.

Giving Serena a mischievous look, Mrs Tonetti murmured, 'Now for it! Don't worry about our being the last to arrive, Jordan knows I tire easily. We'll only stay an hour or so, just so everybody sees you.' She gave Serena an apologetic look. 'Of course,

45

my dear, if you're enjoying yourself we'll stay longer.'

As they walked down a long richly carpeted corridor, Serena hastily replied, 'I shall be quite ready to leave whenever you are. I'll be on tenterhooks in case I say the wrong thing,' adding tentatively, 'I rather feel it might be better if I acted dumb, you know.'

Mrs Tonetti looked slightly alarmed at this pronouncement, and Serena grinned. 'Perhaps what I should have said was quiet, not talkative, I mean.'

The increasing volume of music told Serena they were almost at their destination, and they were. The double doors of the large room opened on to a galaxy of colour. All the colours of the rainbow seemed to be represented by the gowns worn by the women, their displayed jewellery flashing as they were pirouetted round the dance floor by their no less resplendently dressed partners.

As she entered the room Serena felt slightly bemused. The ballroom was magnificent and dated back several centuries, although one would never have realised this by its present décor. The walls were hung with rich tapestry depicting scenes of what Serena presumed to be the island's history. One huge exquisite chandelier hung from the centre of the ceiling, its glittering light throwing out sparks that scintillated over a deep purple, intricately moulded ceiling, giving it a fascinating pattern no decorator could hope to emulate.

Although many of the guests were dancing to the strains of a waltz played by a small orchestra seated on a dais at the end of the vast room, Serena could feel the curiosity their entrance had aroused, and was sure Mrs Tonetti was just as aware of it as she was, for she laid a comforting hand on Serena's arm and led her down the room.

The carefree attitude Serena had talked herself into in the car on the way to the ball deserted her, and the pangs of nervousness returned with interest. Her throat felt dry and she was absolutely certain she would ruin the whole plan within minutes of her entry. She couldn't understand why they all seemed to be staring at her. She swallowed hastily and chided herself for her heightened sensitivity. The trouble was she had a guilty conscience and was dramatising the whole thing, and if she didn't pull herself together soon she really would spoil everything. After giving herself a good talking to, she was almost composed by the time they reached a small knot of people and the first introductions began.

Mrs Tonetti was greeted with much enthusiasm, and remarks were made such as how nice it was to see her at a social function. After solicitous inquiries about her health had been exhausted, Serena was introduced. She shook hands with them and before a general topic of conversation could be introduced, found herself whisked away by Mrs Tonetti and on to the next group.

The initial skirmish over, Serena began to relax. She had to hand it to Mrs Tonetti, whose timing proved masterly, and who she rather suspected was having the time of her life if the wicked twinkle in her eyes as she met them on their way to join yet another small batch of folk was anything to go by!

Serena didn't know when she first became aware of the scrutiny, but as she was led from group to group and small talk developed, a definite sense of being watched gradually bored into her consciousness. At first she thought she had imagined it, there were so many curious stares in her direction, but the feeling persisted so strongly she found herself glancing across the room if only to satisfy herself that her nerves were playing tricks on her, and found herself meeting the gaze of a tall man with reddish-gold hair, and she hastily looked away again. So she hadn't imagined it. With an effort she pulled her thoughts away from the man who was subjecting her to that microscopic examination and tried to concentrate on the conversation around her. She found this harder than she had thought, for a feeling of unease had crept into her senses and even though she smiled and answered a question posed by a frankly admiring young man on whether she would grant him the first dance when all the introductions were over, she was still very much aware of the stranger across the room.

It did occur to her that the man might have met her in London at one of her mother's charity balls, and if this were so, she only hoped he did not know her mother, because if he did the whole thing would go up in smoke. She bit her lip and wished she could have a few minutes alone with Mrs Tonetti and warn her of this possibility.

However, Serena was given no opportunity of communicating her fears as they had now begun the round of introductions on the other side of the room. Serena was just receiving a compliment from a portly man with a strong American accent when she heard Mrs Tonetti exclaim, 'Jordan dear, do come and meet Serena.'

Serena turned smilingly towards the newcomer and almost gasped when she found herself meeting the gaze of the man whose earlier attention had so discomfited her. His voice was deep and well-modulated and as far as looks went he was quite the handsomest man she had ever met, but Serena took particular note of the fact that his smile did not reach his eyes. They were rather striking eyes of a grey-green colour, more green than grey, she decided, and about as cold as an arctic winter.

As her hand was lost in the large strong one offered, she felt a stab of disappointment. She had been so sure she would like Jordan Kerr, but she didn't. She knew she had no right to judge him on first acquaintance and reminded herself he had been very good to Mrs Tonetti and that was really all that mattered, so when he requested the dance that was just starting Serena did not hesitate in accepting, although she knew she had promised the first dance to someone else, but she felt under the circumstances the young man in question would understand, for Jordan Kerr was, after all, her host.

When they began to dance, Serena found his hold tentative, yet not so. After the first few steps she felt as if there were a brick wall between them. His clasp on her hand was light and she received the distinct impression he would have preferred to have kept his distance.

She was a little perplexed by this treatment. As an exceptionally attractive woman, she found his attitude intriguing, to say the least. She stole a quick look at him under her lashes and saw that his features were stiff; he was plainly not enjoying the dance. For one brief second she wondered if he were shy, then instantly dismissed the thought. He was too self-assured to have such a charge levelled at him. Was it reserve? she wondered. Was he so intent on preserving his bachelor status? She almost grinned at this thought. He was so good-looking, and by all accounts wealthy, he had probably been driven to adopt such tactics. Women, she mused, would find him a definite challenge. She remembered the gossip snip she had read about him and wondered if Myrna Simpson had managed to get under his armour. One thing she did know about him, he was no playboy. A man's man, if ever she saw one.

Serena was so immersed in her thoughts that she actually jumped when he suddenly asked, 'Did you get tired of Beroni, or was it mutual?'

She was so surprised that she missed a step and almost cannoned into him, but an expert side step of his prevented the collision. Serena wondered whether she had heard aright and felt like shaking her head. Who on earth was Beroni? She cast about in her mind for some connection of the name with the fashion world, but failed. Her heart sank. It was all very well for Mrs Tonetti, she thought miserably. It appeared this was something she had not clued her up on. Deciding to play safe, she answered airily, 'Oh, it was mutual,' and hoped she had plumped for the right answer.

Judging by the way he retreated back into his ivory tower again, Serena presumed he was satisfied. She almost sighed with relief—that had been a close thing; she must somehow have a private word with Mrs Tonetti and find out what he had been talking about before she really put her foot in it.

When the dance ended, Serena knew relief, for Jordan Kerr's sake as well as her own. Neither of them had enjoyed the duty dance, for that was what it had obviously been. With studious politeness he escorted her back to Mrs Tonetti and excused himself shortly afterwards.

From then on the evening flew by for her. There was no opportunity of a quiet word with Mrs Tonetti, for as she had predicted, Serena found herself inundated with dancing partners. Returning after a succession of dances, Serena found her in the company of an elderly woman, and one glance at the expression on Mrs Tonetti's face told Serena the woman's name. Mrs Simpson was introduced, and it was not long before Serena found herself in complete agreement with Mrs Tonetti's point of view. The woman was dictatorial, inquisitive and, Serena suspected, the worst kind of snob.

Her small black eyes darted over Serena's dress and Serena knew she was mentally pricing it. Her voice was high-pitched and grating. 'Myrna's here somewhere, you know. We ought to have been here earlier, but the flight was delayed. Myrna insists on doing her shopping in New York. We nearly didn't make the ball.' She peered over at the dancers. 'Oh, there she is!' There was a note of satisfaction in her voice. 'Jordan's making up for lost time, I see.'

Serena glanced to where Mrs Simpson was looking and received a slight shock. Jordan Kerr was dancing with a fair girl—fair in every sense of the word. Mrs Tonetti had not really done her justice, Serena thought as she watched them dancing. They made a delightful pair—the girl so slight and utterly feminine, and the tall, broad-shouldered man.

It was the man who held Serena's attention, and

she found it hard to believe that it was the same man who had partnered her earlier, no longer withdrawn and haughty, but now smiling down at the girl in his arms. Had she been closer, Serena was sure that his eyes would be laughing too. She felt a twinge of anger against Jordan Kerr—so he was interested in Miss Simpson; the gossip columns had been right, but it hardly excused the frigid welcome he had extended to her.

Serena's thoughts were interrupted by Mrs Tonetti's abrupt, 'He's already danced with Serena. The poor child hasn't had a moment to herself, but I knew how it would be,' she added a little maliciously.

'Jordan,' Mrs Simpson determinedly pointed out, 'practically pounced on Myrna as soon as we arrived.'

'But he's such a sweet man, isn't he?' purred Mrs Tonetti in swift reply. 'Hates anyone to be left out.'

Somewhere, thought Serena, a bell ought to be rung for seconds out! She was very much afraid her champion was backing a loser if she hoped Serena would steal some of Myrna's thunder. She had not only left the haughty Jordan Kerr cold, but positively icy!

Fortunately supper was then announced, and whatever remark Mrs Simpson had been about to retaliate with was never uttered. With a look of pure disdain she went in search of a bosom friend of hers.

'She has two days' news to catch up on,' Mrs Ton-etti told Serena with twinkling eyes. 'Poor Beryl Johnson's terrified of her, for she bullies her shamefully.' She placed a hand on Serena's arm. 'Shall we find some refreshment, dear? I must say I could do with a nice iced drink.' She smiled at a young man who had partnered Serena earlier, now hovering hesitantly near them and obviously wanting to escort Serena to the buffet room. 'Would you care to join us, Gerald?'

The request was received with a grateful smile and the offer of an arm to each lady. Serena would have preferred to take supper with Mrs Tonetti alone. If Jordan Kerr felt another duty dance was called for later in the evening, there were a few things Serena needed to know, such as who this mysterious Mr Beroni was!

A cold buffet was laid out in the supper room, and various dishes of enticing-looking food were arranged on a long table running the length of the room. Gorgeous floral displays filled spaces in between the dishes, turning an ordinary cold buffet into a work of art. Serena thought it was a pity to disturb it.

Even with such an array of tempting food, Serena was not particularly hungry, but she allowed the said Gerald to place a few exotic-looking pastries on her plate. Mrs Tonetti did not partake, but an iced drink was secured for her.

There were individual tables and chairs scattered about the room so that the food could be consumed in some degree of comfort, and seeing Mrs Tonetti's lips thin after a look down the room, Serena followed her glance and saw Myrna Simpson sitting with Jordan Kerr and was certain Mrs Tonetti was disappointed that he had not joined them for supper.

Serena had a guilty feeling she had let Mrs Tonetti down, which was ridiculous; it was hardly her fault that Jordan Kerr's affections were bespoken, and, she thought a trifle wryly, hardly Myrna's fault that she had such an unlovable grandmother! However, when several other unattached young men found an excuse to join them, making a table for four do duty for six, Serena felt a little vindicated, and Mrs Tonetti was clearly pleased with the way things were going.

The talk was general and very gay. Probes were put out as to how long Serena was staying on the island, and a general lowering of spirits when they were told the date of her departure.

'Surely,' asked a fair young man named Don, 'you could stretch it a bit longer. What's New York got, that we haven't?' he appealed to Mrs Tonetti. 'Couldn't you persuade her to stay on for a while?'

Mrs Tonetti gave a rueful smile. 'I only wish she would. I'm going to try my best, anyway.'

Serena looked up, startled at this reply, Mrs Tonetti knew very well she had to be on that Saturday flight.

Meeting her eyes, Mrs Tonetti smiled apologetically at her. 'Forgive an old lady's selfishness, Serena. Of course you have to go.' She patted her hand and turned to the disappointed admirers. 'But she'll be back, you know. And next time she will stay longer, won't you, Serena?'

There was not much Serena could say to that, apart from agreeing, which she did. She only knew she wanted to come back, and very soon.

The deep voice coming from behind her did not startle her at all, for she had felt his presence long before he spoke.

'Now don't overdo it, Esme. Jake's standing by whenever you've had enough.'

Mrs Tonetti smiled up at the man standing behind Serena. 'Thank you, Jordan dear. To be honest I did think of leaving after supper. It's been a lovely evening, hasn't it, Serena?'

Serena echoed these sentiments, only too pleased that the evening had come to an end. Now there was only one more day to play out the role, and next time, she told herself, she would stick to her adopted grandmother's side like glue and avoid a repetition of further awkward questions.

Her relief was shortlived, for with some trepidation she heard Jordan Kerr smoothly suggest that she stayed on—it was a pity to deprive her of the rest of the evening's entertainment; he would see her safely back, etc.

Serena cast a look of desperation at Mrs Tonetti, who appeared to be wavering. 'It's very kind of you,' she answered hastily before Mrs Tonetti could speak. 'I've only been here a day or so,' she lied, 'and travelling always tires me, I'm quite ready to leave when Nan does.'

She was quite surprised the way the name 'Nan' came so readily, as she had anticipated having trouble over it, and thanked her lucky stars she had been alert enough to use it. She had to crane her neck to look up at Jordan towering above her, and knew by the slightly altered mouth line that he was not pleased with this information. Well, it couldn't be helped, she thought, and there was nothing he could do about it. But she soon found she had misjudged him.

'Come now,' he said a little silkily, and to her sensitive ears a little challengingly. 'You don't expect me to believe that, do you? Surely you're used to travel?' He glanced back at Mrs Tonetti. 'I appeal to you, Esme. I expect Serena is being extra thoughtful on your behalf, don't you?'

Mrs Tonetti got quite carried away, and Serena could see why; Mrs Simpson was standing a little way away and was taking more than a passing interest in the conversation. Basking in the light of success, Mrs Tonetti ignored the plain S.O.S.

Serena's eyes were sending her. Jordan had shown an interest in Serena, and all else was forgotten.

However, Serena was not beaten yet. 'I do assure you, I am tired,' she insisted, fixing a look of 'don't you dare leave me' on Mrs Tonetti.

'Nonsense, child!' Mrs Tonetti exclaimed. 'Jordan is quite right. Why shouldn't you enjoy yourself? I shall go straight to bed when I get home, anyway. So you stay, my dear. I know I can rely on Jordan to see you safely back.'

Serena was not even given the chance of a hasty few words with her before she left, as her wrap was immediately sent for, and Jake appeared saying that the car was waiting, leaving Serena feeling like a shipwrecked mariner cast ashore on a desert island.

CHAPTER FOUR

As soon as Mrs Tonetti was out of sight Gerald, determined to steal a march on his rivals, asked Serena to dance. His reign was short, for as soon as the dance was over an apprehensive Serena found Jordan Kerr waiting to claim the next one. With a smooth, 'Excuse me, old chap,' to Gerald, he whisked her on to the floor for a quickstep.

The impression she had received before was even more pronounced this time, and Serena wished she could define it. They were dancing, yes, but they might have been on opposite sides of the room. Partly to relieve her tension she attempted to make conversation. 'I do appreciate your concern for my grandmother,' she said quietly, and smiled up at him.

The smile was not returned; if anything, he seemed to freeze a degree lower. 'Do you?' he answered coldly.

The answer completely nonplussed Serena, who decided to give up. She had tried, hadn't she? What an exceedingly odd man he was. Perhaps he had a thing about brunettes! Out of the corner of her eye she caught sight of Gerald hovering by the side of the dance floor and knew he was waiting for an opportunity to claim the next dance. The sight gave her some consolation; whatever effect she had on Jordan Kerr she was grateful it was not catching! The thought made her smile.

'Something amusing you?' asked Jordan Kerr haughtily.

Serena glanced up at him. Now she was angry and her eyes showed her feelings, but she answered airily enough, 'Just a passing thought, Mr Kerr.'

When the dance ended, Serena, meaning to show this autocratic man that she did not require any more attention from him, if it could be called that, murmured, 'If you'll excuse me,' and made a move to pass him.

As if she had not spoken, he asked abruptly, 'Are you interested in past history?'

Serena stared at him. Now what? Was he making an effort to entertain her for Mrs Tonetti's sake? She wished she could state quite categorically that she was not a bit interested in history and end the uncomfortable interlude for both of them, but she knew she was under an obligation. She had promised to help Mrs Tonetti, although, she thought darkly, the said lady really didn't deserve any such consideration, not after deserting her like that, throwing her as it were into the lion's den. She corrected that last thought on noticing the way Jordan Kerr was watching her with those extraordinary eyes of his, now more green than grey. Panther's eyes, she thought, and almost shivered.

She was quite at a loss to understand why he should want to discuss such a subject, then she remembered the Centenary. He was probably very proud of his ancestors, and the fact that she had made a point of attending the celebrations would, from his point of view, mean she was interested. Besides, she mused, it would take his mind off other matters—such as this Mr Beroni, and any other tricky questions he might throw at her.

'Well, yes,' she replied, managing to produce a bright smile at him. 'I'm afraid I don't know a lot about the island's history. It's very kind of you ...'

Before she had completed the sentence Serena found herself being guided out of the ballroom and down a long corridor, and it occurred to her that no matter what her answer had been she would still be taking this walk. She tried to quell the waves of apprehension flowing through her and told herself she was just being fanciful again. Really, she was just not cut out for this kind of masquerade.

When they reached the end of the corridor Jordan Kerr opened a door on his left and indicated that she should precede him into the room. Doing so, Serena found herself in a large room that was obviously a study. Her eyes rested on a handsome mahogany desk placed near a large bay window, then to the bookshelves that took up the whole of one wall. Her fears were now dispelled, for this would be where the books on the island's history were kept; the maps too, she thought, as her eye caught sight of an ancient-looking map framed and hung on the wall behind the desk.

Jordan Kerr closed the door behind him and selecting a chair picked it up and placed it in front of the desk. Sitting down behind the desk, he silently gestured Serena to the chair in front of him.

A variety of thoughts flashed through Serena's mind, most of them alarming. She looked at the cold handsome face of the man seated in front of her. This was no pleasant tête-à-tête, in fact it looked more in the nature of an inquisition!

Serena thought she had the answer—Mrs Tonetti had not fooled him for one moment—he knew she was an impostor! Did he think she was some kind of adventuress and meant to warn her off? She felt a kind of relief, for she would now have to tell him the whole story. She was sure Mrs Tonetti would understand and she was also sure Jordan Kerr would respect Mrs Tonetti's odd but very understandable duplicity.

Having worked it all out in her mind Serena relaxed and sat back in her chair, then looked up to meet those strange eyes closely watching her; she smiled at him and was a little disturbed to see no change of expression on his face. This was a new experience for Serena, for her smiles usually worked wonders.

'We shall dispense with the pleasantries, if you please,' Jordan Kerr said in an intimidating voice. 'Also with the fancy name you've bestowed upon yourself.' He shot her a look of disdain. 'I suppose you found it in one of the society magazines?'

Without giving Serena a chance to answer, he continued, 'I shall address you by your real name. Under the circumstances, I hardly feel the name Serena is suitable.' He leaned forward towards her, his long sensitive fingers spread out on the desk top. 'So—Miss Tonetti, we meet at last!'

Serena did not like the look in his eyes as he said this and lowered hers to concentrate on those hands. Strong hands, she thought absently.

'I must say you're running true to form,' his voice held disgust. 'I rather expected you to turn up around now. I hope you note,' he said silkily, 'that I have not asked you why you're here. I know why. In fact, Miss Tonetti, there isn't much I don't know about you, so I'm afraid for once you're going to find those smiles of yours are wasted. How did you find out about your grandmother?' he suddenly shot out at her, and again giving Serena no chance to answer he carried on, 'With someone like you there would be ways and means, wouldn't there? I see you've managed to ingratiate yourself with the right people. Running quite high, aren't you?'

His glance flicked over her dress and Serena knew he had correctly priced it. She was getting a little tired of this one-sided conversation and decided it was time she made some contribution, if only to get things straight. 'There's something you ought to know,' she said quickly. 'My name really is Serena Belmont. I . . .' She cast him a look of bewilderment. 'I simply have no idea what you're talking about.' She frowned, then added hesitantly, 'Whatever it is, it appears to be of a personal nature concerning Mrs Tonetti, and I find myself in an embarrassing position.' Her lovely eyes were wide as she met the enigmatic eyes of Jordan Kerr. She sighed. 'I apologise for the deception, but I do assure you that Mrs Tonetti approached me a few days ago and asked me to——' Here she faltered. What could she say? That she had agreed to act out a figment of an old lady's imagination?—only it wasn't imagination, the granddaughter did exist—not only did she exist, but she had apparently made a formidable enemy of the man now seated opposite her.

Serena swallowed; no matter how mad it sounded she had to tell the truth. She began again. 'When Mrs Tonetti asked me to pretend to be her granddaughter I had no idea that a granddaughter existed—In fact, I was led to believe that she was alone in the world. It seemed harmless at the time,' she commented. 'However, it appears to have backfired.'

Jordan Kerr leaned back in his chair and studied her with hooded eyes. Serena had a nasty feeling he hadn't believed a word of her story, and she was right; his next words proved it.

'I understand you were leaving on Saturday,' he said offhandedly, completely disregarding her explanation.

Serena wondered what he meant by 'were'. She met his gaze levelly. 'I leave for New York on Saturday,' she confirmed hoping the information would please him. There was no doubt that Miss Tonetti was not welcome on his island.

'I said, "were", Miss Tonetti, and I meant exactly that,' he said harshly.

Serena stared at him and meeting his haughty glance felt a stab of temper. Who did he think he was, anyway? She had told him the truth and he wasn't even going to give her the chance of proving her identity.

Her lovely eyes flashed shoots of violet blue as her temper rose. She wasn't going to take any more from this man. She stood up, her slim shoulders straight, and angrily brushed away a stray tendril of hair that clung to her cheek. 'And I said I was leaving on Saturday,' she said coldly. 'Furthermore, I see no point in going on with this conversation. I am not used to being called a liar,' she added haughtily as she swung round towards the door. She did not wait for his answer and with her head held high walked to the door and attempted to open it, but it remained closed; it was locked!

She turned furiously to face the man calmly watching her. 'Unlock this door at once! Do you hear?' she commanded. 'Or I'll scream the place down!'

To Serena's further fury she saw him smile, and it wasn't a pleasant smile, nor was the look in his eyes. She felt the first pangs of fear. He was mad! He must be!

'I must congratulate you on a fine performance,' he drawled. 'By all means scream if you want to. The room is soundproofed—however, I don't advise you to try. I'm in no mood for hysterics and I don't think you'd care for the remedial treatment. Now stop this play-acting and come and sit down.' He glanced at his hands now lightly drumming the desk top. 'I realise all this must have come as a shock to you; you hardly expected anyone to know your past. indiscretions, did you? let alone force you to make some amendment.'

Serena's eyes opened yet wider. What had she walked into? And what exactly did he mean by 'amendment'? She made herself remain calm, although she wanted to scream at him that she knew nothing and it was all a ghastly mistake.

'Sit down,' he ordered. 'This is going to be a long session. You leave when we come to an understanding, and not before. The sooner you realise you're no longer dealing with a frail, sick woman,' again his voice held disgust, 'your grandmother, no less,' he thundered as his fist hit the desk top making Serena jump. 'Did you ever give her one thought in those five years?' he ground out. 'Did you know what you did when you stole those bonds?'

Serena went pale—she was shocked, and it shone out of her eyes.

Seeing her stunned reaction, Jordan Kerr nodded grimly. 'Oh, yes, I know it all—every sordid little detail, and I only wish I'd known at the time; it would have been a different story if I had. You wouldn't have got far, even with Beroni's help.' He shrugged. 'As it was, I didn't hear about it until six months afterwards. Your grandfather tried to cover up for you. He was forced to sell everything he had to pay back those bonds.'

Serena's shocked eyes watched his long slender fingers curl into a ball and saw the knuckles whiten. He was silent for a moment or so, then went on harshly, 'I don't suppose he would have told me then, but he had to throw himself on my charity. Two of those bonds had been mine and he couldn't raise the money in time to redeem them.' His jaw hardened. 'As if I cared a damn about the money! Antonio was my friend; the money meant nothing to me. I eventually got the story out of him, but by that time he was a very sick man. Worry and the effort to raise that amount at such short notice had taken its toll.'

Serena was numb; her legs felt weak; she had to

sit down now. All too clearly did she see what Jordan Kerr was leading up to. She moved slowly towards the chair and sat down wearily on it.

Giving her a contemptuous look, he continued. 'Not a pretty story, is it?' he sneered. 'And I'm going to tell you something else, just to show you that it's no use your pleading youth and ignorance; I took it upon myself to bring you back—I wasn't too sure that you weren't just a headstrong girl swayed by the smooth wooing of Beroni; for that's what your grandfather had convinced himself was the case. He said that if he'd known of the association he would have put a stop to it—but you were both very discreet, weren't you? He only called when your grandparents were otherwise engaged.' He stared at her, his grey green eyes blazing for a moment. 'I suppose he found it hard to believe that an eighteen-year-old girl was capable of robbing her own kith and kin, especially as they had given you a home when your parents died.'

Apart from a sense of shock, Serena was horribly embarrassed; this was none of her business. She wished she could make him stop, but she knew she couldn't, and she felt sick.

The voice ground on, 'But I found different, didn't I? Beroni was a babe in arms compared to you! After following your somewhat unsavoury trail from hotel to hotel, and finally the not so flash boarding houses, I couldn't stomach any more. I had meant to restore you,' his voice grew harder, 'back to the bosom of your family, as it were. It would have been some consolation to a broken man who I knew hadn't much time left. However, I came to the conclusion that they were better off without you. You were a tramp!'

Serena's startled eyes flew to his and his lips thinned as he met that look. 'I make no apology. You might as well know where you stand right now. I know what you are; those wide-eyed looks are lost on me. Having met you at last, I do however now realise how you've managed to survive. With your looks you'd have no trouble in arousing sympathy from the male species. You weren't fussy, after all, were you? I found out you'd dropped Beroni soon after you'd landed in England. He'd served his purpose, hadn't he? and you probably felt you could do better for yourself.'

He nodded towards her dress. 'And you did, didn't you? But you couldn't resist seeing whether there were any pickings left this end, could you? And that's where you made your first mistake. As I said, I'd been expecting you, although I found it hard to believe you'd have the gall to attempt a reconciliation with your grandmother. Seems I underestimated you—you had the gall, all right!'

Feeling as if she were in the middle of a nightmare, Serena said faintly, 'Please stop. You're making a dreadful mistake. I'm not Lisa Tonetti—I know you don't believe me, but please speak to Mrs Tonetti, she'll tell you the truth when she knows what's happened.'

His fist hit the desk again. 'Do you want another death on your conscience?' he all but shouted at her. 'And don't say you don't know what I'm talking about. You wouldn't have dared come back if she'd known what you'd done. You knew very well your grandfather would have kept quiet about it—he was very fond of you, wasn't he? He made some story up about a slump in stocks—and even if you weren't sure, those notices in the agony columns inserted in all leading papers for months after the death of your grandfather asking you to contact your grandmother would have given you the answer. Oh, yes, you gauged things just right, and I'm warning you, you breathe one word of our conversation to her and I'll have you arrested within hours. Some of those bonds were mine, remember? If you cause your grandmother one moment's further unhappiness, I shall take great pleasure in doing just that.'

Serena's muddled senses tried to sort out the implication of these words, but failed utterly. She had had enough; she couldn't begin to make sense of anything—not now.

'So,' he went on in that toneless voice, 'you will stay. Do you understand? Your grandmother's living on borrowed time anyway. For what time she has left, you'll make her happy, do you hear? You'll be a sweet, considerate granddaughter until the end of her days. She deserves that much from you. You'll cancel that New York booking—or rather I'll cancel it. Don't try to leave or you'll be sorry. I've many business acquaintances in New York and in most other capitals, so your escape will be shortlived, I assure you. I'm a wealthy man and there are ways and means, as I'm sure you know, of getting information, and I'll not hesitate to use any method at my disposal to track you down.'

CHAPTER FIVE

SERENA did not remember the journey back that night; she only knew she was grateful that Mrs Tonetti had gone to bed and she need not face her until the following morning, by which time she hoped she would have gained some measure of composure.

Thankfully closing her bedroom door after refusing Molly's kind offer of a hot drink, Serena leaned weakly against it for support. She still couldn't believe that that traumatic interview had actually taken place. 'I'm dreaming it,' she whispered in the silence of the empty room, and shook her head bewilderedly. It simply couldn't be true—any of it. Jordan Kerr looked sane, but he obviously was not. For some reason he had taken a dislike to her and had thought up some ridiculous story to frighten her with. Her lips straightened; she was not so easily frightened. Her palpitating heart told her otherwise and she swallowed hastily, then took a deep breath.

It was all very well trying to convince herself Jordan Kerr was mad when she knew very well he was not; he was horribly, coldly sane. Her brow creased; but if he was sane why had he made such outrageous accusations against someone he had admitted he had never met? Her fingers curled into a ball. A tramp, he'd called her. She bit her lip—no, not her; Lisa Tonetti.

With legs that felt like rubber she walked over to the dressing table and with fingers that shook took out the small snap she had found earlier that evening in the drawer. For a while she stared at it, then with an impatient shrug put it back again. It was just a photograph of a girl. It couldn't tell her anything apart from the fact that the girl could have been herself, but wasn't.

Sinking wearily into a chair, Serena was forced to admit to herself that she was in a predicament and the sooner she pulled herself together and brought some cold logic into the situation, the sooner a sensible answer would present itself. Her lips twisted wryly when she thought of how she had felt that very morning; how she had wanted to do just what Jordan Kerr had ordered her to do—stay on the island. She frowned; she had wanted an excuse to cut herself free from Roger's determined attentions, but not this way. Her frown deepened; in any other circumstances she would have entered into the spirit of the thing, but even if she had wanted to see it through, it wouldn't work; Roger would see to that.

Her eyes narrowed. Jordan Kerr didn't know about Roger. Serena almost smiled; she only hoped to be present when the confrontation took place. It would give her some consolation to see the autocratic Jordan Kerr stopped dead in his tracks. She tried to imagine him actually apologising to her, but failed to bring the scene to life. He would be more likely to give her a lecture on her stupidity of agreeing to pose as Lisa Tonetti.

The name brought back the ordeal she had recently gone through and with it an uncomfortable feeling that things weren't going to be that straightforward. For instance, she mused; just how ill was Mrs Tonetti? Serena recalled the short walk to the hotel and her breathlessness, and she had admitted that she had to rest a lot. At this point she remembered Jordan Kerr's remark, 'She's living on borrowed time,' and his harsh, 'Do you want another death on your conscience?' Serena shivered as the truth hit her; heart trouble—it all fitted—in other words a shock could and probably would, kill Mrs Tonetti!

An extremely miserable and apprehensive Serena prepared for bed. Cold logic had only served to emphasize the explosive position she had unwittingly landed herself in. Somehow she had to find a solution to the problem and she devoutly hoped the morning's clear light would provide one.

Serena awoke to the call of birds and lay for a moment or so listening to their shrill cries; she drowsily watched the patterns of sunlight filter through the sunblinds and play on the deep blue carpet, until Molly tapping on the door and entering with her usual cheery smile and her morning tea broke her spell of contentment.

As she sat up to accept the tea it was as much as she could do to return the smile and try to match Molly's happy observations on the day's forthcoming events.

Listening to her gay chatter while she put her evening dress on a hanger and hung it in the wardrobe, Serena felt a pang of guilt. She ought to have done that herself and not left it to Molly to clear up after her, no matter how weary she had been. She apologised and said she had been rather tired.

Molly received the apology with some surprise, then grinned at Serena. 'My pleasure, Miss Serena,' she said shyly, adding as she left the room, 'Missus happy now. Okay, now you come.'

This gentle observation did nothing to lighten Serena's depression; if anything it only underlined her tenuous position.

While she dressed, Serena rehearsed in her mind what she would tell Mrs Tonetti when she inquired how the rest of the evening had gone. She would particularly want to know how much time Jordan Kerr had spent with her. Serena's fingers stilled in the act of zipping up her dress. How much was it safe to tell her? She was certain that their absence would not have gone unnoticed, particularly by Mrs Simpson, not to mention her granddaughter, Myrna.

Her fingers went cold; supposing Jordan had told Myrna the whole miserable story? He would have to have given her some explanation for deserting her and devoting the rest of the evening to a complete stranger. And if Myrna knew … She closed her eyes; how long before Mrs Simpson got hold of the story? Serena swallowed: it didn't bear thinking about!

When she was ready she made her way to the patio, grateful that she would have at least another hour before her hostess put in an appearance. Perhaps by then the solution that had so far deserted her would come to mind.

On reaching the patio, however, she saw with dismay that Mrs Tonetti had risen early and was waiting to take breakfast with her. In spite of her feelings, Serena managed to answer her bright smile of welcome and sat down wondering how she was going to manage to swallow a cup of coffee, let alone partake any food with her stomach feeling as if it had twisted itself into a knot.

After making solicitous inquiries as to how she had slept, and how she was sure Serena had enjoyed the rest of the evening, Mrs Tonetti lapsed into silence.

Serena was slightly astounded, and far from being grateful for her hostess's lack of interest in the past evening's events, found her preoccupied manner more worrying than the questions she had surmised she would be asked.

Even Serena's lack of appetite went unnoticed, and she was a little grateful for this; above all, she had to act naturally and normally her appetite was a healthy one.

Only after Molly had cleared the table and left a fresh pot of coffee for them did Mrs Tonetti attempt to raise herself out of her reverie long enough to inquire whether Serena would like another cup.

Serena shook her head and sat back watching Mrs Tonetti; instinct told her to hold her tongue and not, as her by now ragged nerves were prompting her to do, cry out that it was all right, she knew the whole story and she wasn't to worry about it.

'If only,' sighed Mrs Tonetti, 'Lisa had been more like you!'

Serena held her breath and felt her pulse quicken. Now it was out! How much did Mrs Tonetti know? Had she guessed the truth? She met her sad eyes half-warily, desperately trying to keep the anxiety out of her own.

'I'm afraid I lied to you, dear,' Mrs Tonetti said quietly. 'You've been so sweet and understanding.' She twitched her finely woven shawl closer to her as if she felt the cold, yet it was a warm morning. Straightening her back, she gave Serena a pleading look. 'I want to tell you about her,' she said firmly, 'and ask you to forgive me—although,' she said softly, 'I'm sure you'll know I didn't really mean to deceive you.' She hesitated. 'It's only that if you'd

77

known Lisa really did exist, you wouldn't have agreed to help me. You wouldn't have understood, you see, that there's no likelihood of her ever coming back.'

A stab of apprehension flowed through Serena; she was now certain Mrs Tonetti knew the whole miserable story. 'Please,' she said quickly, 'it doesn't matter, you know. Whatever it is, I'm sure it's very personal, and,' she added a little desperately, 'I am enjoying myself. I wanted an excuse to stay here, remember? and honestly I'm very grateful to you.'

Mrs Tonetti continued to gaze at her with those sad eyes of hers and with a sinking heart Serena knew she had failed to divert her from the subject.

The old lady patted Serena's arm and smiled. 'And I want you to go on enjoying yourself,' she said gently. 'However, I want to tell you about Lisa— you see, there hasn't been anyone I could talk to about her. It isn't easy, you know, explaining why your only grandchild doesn't come to see you.'

She was silent for a moment or so and her gaze left Serena and centred on the panoramic view before them, but Serena knew she was not seeing the view. Miserably she knew that short of a sudden earthquake, there was nothing she could do to prevent Mrs Tonetti reliving the unhappy past.

'I'd better go back to the start,' Mrs Tonetti began wearily. 'That way you'll understand how things were. Antonio and I had only one child, a son.' She broke off again as if assembling her thoughts and Serena longed to interrupt and tell her it didn't matter, she didn't want to know, but she couldn't; it would only upset Mrs Tonetti and might make things worse.

'I'm afraid Antonio and Michele hadn't a lot in common,' she continued sadly. 'In a way, I don't suppose I helped matters by spoiling Michele. I used to think Antonio was too hard on the boy and I tried to make up for it,' she sighed. 'Antonio always intended that Michele should follow him in the family business. He was an accountant, you know, and a very successful one, only——' she hesitated, 'he made a bad investment just before we retired, and things weren't easy.'

Inwardly Serena breathed a sigh of relief. She wasn't going to hear about Lisa's treachery. It looked as if Jordan Kerr had been right and she did not know the true facts.

'But this, of course, was a long time afterwards,' went on Mrs Tonetti, sounding impatient with herself for her slight deviation. 'As I said, Michele and his father were always at loggerheads, and after one particularly sharp disagreement Michele slammed out of the house.' There was another tiny silence, then Mrs Tonetti swallowed quickly and continued, 'We didn't hear from him until three years later. He told us he was married and wanted to patch things up; I was delighted, of course; I even had hopes of him agreeing to settle down and take his exams. He was only twenty-one, you know, and had passed his prelims before the flare-up with his father.'

She fingered her shawl agitatedly and Serena wished she could hurry her through this painful period of her life.

'But it didn't work out,' she said quietly. 'He did come back and he brought his wife with him. It didn't help matters when we found the girl was well advanced in pregnancy.' She smiled apologetically at Serena. 'I do apologise, dear, but you must see how things were, or you wouldn't understand—you see, Antonio had a strict upbringing—good Italian families have, you know, and it was quite obvious that Michele had had to marry the girl.' Her hand twitched her shawl again. 'I don't think I'd ever seen Antonio so furious.' She sighed. 'Even then, I do believe things would have worked out if Michele had really wanted to settle down and join his father in the firm—or at least, have had a try at it—but all he wanted was money; and I must confess neither Antonio or I cared much for the girl he had married. It soon became very obvious that they were not in love and the girl had married him in the expectation of a wealthy future. At that time, you see, we were quite well off.

'So we come to Lisa.' She looked at Serena. 'It's hard to believe that two girls could look so alike, yet be so very different—you're all I wanted her to be.' She nodded gently. 'You are like her in looks, Serena. I did tell the truth when I told you that, apart from your eyes. Lisa's were dark blue, not that lovely violet colour of yours.' She sighed. 'And she was harder than you are, even when she was seventeen I saw that. That was how old she was when we first saw her, you know. She just turned up and told us who she was. We didn't even know whether Michele's child had been a boy or girl, for after Antonio had given him the money he wanted, he told him there wouldn't be any more payments like that. Either he came back and joined the firm, or got himself a steady job of some kind—whichever it was, he'd have to earn the next amount.' The hand clutching the shawl tightened, showing the almost transparent veins on her thin hands. 'We never heard from him again,' she swallowed. 'Lisa told us her father had died when she was fifteen.' Her voice had a weary bitterness in it. 'Her mother apparently, didn't bother to inform us.'

Serena interrupted quickly, hoping to get Mrs Tonetti's thoughts away from that memory. 'And Lisa's mother?' she asked.

Mrs Tonetti nodded. 'That's why Lisa came to find us. Her mother had told her that if anything happened to her, she was to come to us.' Her eyes moistened. 'I really thought that at last,' she closed her eyes. 'We did everything to make her happy, spoilt her shamelessly—you see, in our way we tried to make up for the past. There were faults on both sides, and there had been too much bitterness.' Her smile was bitter-sweet. 'Antonio spoilt her even more than I did,' her voice faltered. 'But it didn't work. I'm afraid she became infatuated with a married man.' She made a small moue of distaste. 'Not a very nice man, either.'

Again there was a small silence and Serena hoped she had come to the end of her narrative, but there was more.

'Everything seemed to happen at once,' Mrs Tonetti sighed. 'Lisa running away with this man, then the bad news about our finances. Antonio wasn't a young man, and he ought to have retired a year before, but there was no one to carry on the firm, you see, and he was reluctant to sell the practice. He never really got over it, it wasn't only the financial worry. I think he blamed himself for not keeping a stricter eye on Lisa's activities; he'd grown extremely fond of her during that year she was with us.'

Knowing the real cause of Mr Tonetti's unhappiness, Serena wondered how anyone could be callous enough to do what Lisa Tonetti had done.

The thin tired voice went on, 'I tried to find her, you know, after Antonio's death. I advertised for months, not only in Italy, but in England too. All to no avail; in the end I was forced to come to the conclusion that we meant nothing to her. It's been five years, and I've not even had a postcard from her. If it hadn't been for a friend of ours who actually saw her in London three years ago, I might have wondered whether she'd met with some accident.'

'Perhaps——' began Serena gently, meaning to point out that she had been mistaken for Lisa herself and that it hadn't been Lisa but someone else.

Mrs Tonetti forestalled her with a sad smile. 'Oh, yes, dear, it was Lisa. Mrs Carstairs saw her quite plainly and actually called out to her, she was only across the street from her. She told me Lisa had looked up quickly to see who was calling her and then deliberately walked away in the opposite direction.'

Serena was effectively silenced until another thought struck her. Surely, if Lisa Tonetti were as avaricious as Jordan Kerr had intimated, wouldn't she have tried to make a comeback when the money ran out? She didn't know how much was involved, a goodly amount if she had managed to survive for five years on it, she thought dryly, then she remembered something else. Jordan Kerr had said she had left Beroni as soon as they reached England. That meant whatever amount was involved would have to be split two ways. He had also said something about following her trail from the good class hotels to the not so good boarding houses, so unless Lisa was reserving her resources, it didn't make sense. She frowned, then asked suddenly, 'Does Lisa know where you are now, do you think?'

Again she received that sad smile from Mrs Tonetti. 'Yes, dear,' she said gently. 'It was often discussed that we would come here for our retirement years. We used to spend our vacations here every year, but when Lisa was with us we decided to go to Paris instead, she was so keen to go there, and there isn't really much in the way of entertainment for young people here, you know. Jordan doesn't cater for tourism, he doesn't encourage it nor discourage it, but if they come here in the hopes of "living it up" then I'm afraid they're soon disappointed. There are no gambling casinos here, or cinemas. The only concession Jordan's made in that line is in nightclubs, and really they're more in the nature of a late-night restaurant, no floor shows, as it were.'

Her question answered, Serena saw a chance to steer the conversation away from the unhappy past to the present, and she quickly asked about the Centenary. 'It's more than a hundred years, of course, isn't it?' she queried. 'Since the landing, I mean.'

To her relief, her tactics worked. Mrs Tonetti frowned in concentration for a moment. 'I think it's the fourth, dear. I believe it took place in the sixteenth century.' She glanced at her wrist watch. 'Good gracious, is that the time? Thank goodness you reminded me. We must get ready at once. Jordan's sending a car to collect us and it will be here in fifteen minutes.'

Before she entered her bedroom, Mrs Tonetti reminded Serena to take a hat of some kind. 'It gets quite hot, and we shall be standing about on the beach for quite a while.'

CHAPTER SIX

SERENA changed into a turquoise linen trouser suit with a sleeveless tunic and lime green organdie long-sleeved blouse, that would let whatever breeze there was to be had filter through to her.

Her one and only hat was a wide-brimmed white straw she had bought specifically for the cruise. Unlike her mother, Serena did not care for hats and only wore them under protest, but she knew from past experience that unless she could produce one she would be prevailed upon to wear one of her mother's. To Mrs Belmont, hats were a vital part of her ensemble, and Serena had once heard her declare that she felt undressed without one! Of course, there were hats, and hats; her mother's always seemed to consist of a concoction of frippery dreamed up by a designer with surrealistic tendencies!

As she placed the hat on her head, Serena's thoughts went from her mother to Roger and his reaction to the news that she would not be joining them for the cruise. Meeting her reflection in the mirror she paled; he would be simply furious! Serena had an idea of what he had planned for the culmination of the cruise—an engagement ring on her finger! She was also sure he had already bought the ring, ready to slip it on her third finger when he had worn her down.

Her even white teeth caught her bottom lip; she couldn't see Roger leaving it at that. He would come, she knew he would. It wouldn't be too difficult for him to find out where she was staying. In her mind's eye she saw him arriving at the chalet demanding to know the reason why she had cancelled the cruise. She sighed; even the enterprising Mrs Tonetti would be hard put to it to think up a plausible excuse at such short notice. Of course, thought Serena, she could warn her, but that wouldn't get them anywhere either. She could hardly see him condoning her well-meaning, but as it had turned out, foolish duplicity. Neither could Serena see him agreeing to respect the confidential news about Mrs Tonetti's state of health, particularly when he heard about Jordan Kerr!

Depression settled on her like a cloud; the meeting between Roger and Jordan Kerr which she had envisaged with so much pleasure the previous evening now loomed on the horizon as Mrs Tonetti's death knell—Serena shivered. There was nothing for it but for her to leave on Saturday. Somehow she must make Jordan Kerr see that. If he really wanted to protect Mrs Tonetti he had to be made to see it.

The car drew up just as Serena joined Mrs Tonetti in the lounge. Mrs Tonetti had also changed and wore a heavy silk navy blue suit with matching straw hat. Smiling at Serena, she commented, 'You're going to enjoy this, Serena. Now come along, or we'll miss the landing.'

Following her out of the chalet, Serena thought it all depended on whether she could make a certain individual see sense; if not, Mrs Tonetti's confident prediction would go sadly astray.

She was jerked out of her miserable musings by the awesome sight of a piratical-looking character waiting to convey them to the beach.

Mrs Tonetti chuckled and asked, 'It is you, Jake, isn't it? I suppose if you're taking part in the landing we ought not to keep you waiting.'

Jake grinned and opened the car doors for them. 'Plenty of time, Mrs Tonetti,' he assured her as he seated her in the front seat, then assisted Serena into the back.

Having only seen Jake in the half-light the previous evening, Serena was now able to take in his features. As she had guessed, he was Polynesian, with the warm honey-coloured skin of that race. Her eyes travelled from his smiling face to his apparel, firstly to the bandanna tied tightly round his forehead giving him a slightly villainish look, then moving on to his clothes. His open-throated white blouse-like shirt had full sleeves, and his black breeches were adorned with a brass studded belt. Black plimsoll-type shoes completed the outfit. With a slight start,

Serena realised she was looking at what must be an almost identical copy of the clothes worn by the sea-farers of old, and her gaze centred on the studded belt with its ominous small hooks at each end to hold no doubt the swinging cutlass and lethal dagger. In spite of the heat, she shivered. It was beyond her comprehension that those times should be recalled, let alone celebrated!

It was only a short ride to the beach and when they arrived, instead of following the track down to the beach itself, Jake swung the car on to the slightly elevated ground running parallel to the beach track. For a second, Serena wondered why as they seemed to be heading away from the main sightseeing area, then as they rounded a bend and joined several other cars pulled up a little in front of them, she saw the reason for the diverted course. The whole sweep of the beautiful bay was before them. Not very far below them lay the beach, now crowded to capacity with what Serena presumed to be the entire population of the island, but on catching sight of several people sporting expensive-looking cameras making their way determinedly to the front of the crowd, she amended that last thought to include tourists.

Alighting from the car, they made their way to-wards a row of seating, and Serena, holding Mrs Tonetti's arm to make certain her step was firm on the uneven ground, saw with a start of dismay that among the occupants already seated were Mrs Simpson and Myrna. All her earlier fears crowded in on her; she ought to have known they would be present, but she had somehow imagined a crowd of people among which it would be possible to keep one's distance. Serena had a horrible feeling that nothing—but nothing—was going to go right for her, and she didn't know why she bothered. She might as well give in gracefully and accept whatever fate had been combining to throw at her.

To take her mind off these disturbing thoughts she concentrated on the two figures in front that had prompted her near-hysterical line of reasoning. Myrna, she noticed, also wore a trouser suit; its well-cut navy blue jacket emphasized her slim shoulders. A small flap at the back of the collar with white piping gave it definite naval undertones and the pert navy blue boater that rested on her fair head completed the illusion. Serena's thoughts went back to the previous evening and her brief introduction to her after that nerve-shattering interview in Jordan Kerr's study when they had met her on the way out of the study. She had come to find out what was keeping him so long. Serena had been in no state for polite conversation—not, she thought, that Myrna would have welcomed it. The hand held out after the introduction had been as cold as the look in her light blue eyes.

As they reached the seating Serena gave a thankful sigh that the seats on either side of the Simpsons had just been taken, and she prayed that Mrs Tonetti would choose the seats at the end of the line, thus forestalling any chance of further skirmishing on the two elderly ladies' part.

As if Serena had willed it, Mrs Tonetti did choose the end seating, and after the greetings from the other residents and a cool nod from both the Simpsons, they settled down to watch the proceedings.

Gazing out at the blue expanse of the bay, Serena sent up a little 'thank you' for this first obstacle cleared. Her eyes, resting on a small clump of palms that seemed to form a natural barrier of shelter for the small bay, softened for a moment. It was so beautiful; white foam gently lapped the shore and was almost soporific in its action, Serena felt she wanted nothing more than to be allowed to stay there forever, listening to the sea's eternal lullaby.

Serena's moment of tranquillity was soon over as a sudden movement on her right caught her attention and she glanced across in time to see the tall form of Jordan Kerr effortlessly vault up the slight incline that separated them from the beach.

As she watched him stride towards them she was thankful he had not elected to join the landing party; the very sight of him put her nerves on edge, and she hated to think what effect he would have had on her dressed in pirate's costume. After that first quick glance in his direction, Serena looked straight ahead of her and tried to concentrate on the view that had previously held her attention; but she could still see the man who had forced her into her present predicament. She knew exactly what he wore; the way the blue blazer sat on his wide shoulders and the blue shirt that was open at the neck, even to the dove grey tapered slacks.

Bestowing a lazy bronzed smile on Mrs Tonetti, he asked as he joined them, 'What do you think of the good news?'

Serena cast a wary look towards him, then looked at Mrs Tonetti, who was frankly puzzled, her brows raised in query as she glanced from Serena back to Jordan again.

Feeling the quick warning look Jordan Kerr gave her, Serena's heart sank; he was taking no chances of her backing out.

'I've persuaded your granddaughter to lengthen her stay, haven't I, Serena?' he said smoothly, meeting Serena's smouldering eyes with a glint in his.

Very clever, thought Serena, only he wasn't going to get away with it. Refusing to meet his eyes, she murmured, 'Well, let's say I'm considering it. Nothing,' she said firmly but with a stab of regret as she watched the hope in Mrs Tonetti's eyes slowly fade away, 'has been settled. And,' she added brightly, 'there'll be other times, won't there, Nan?' she appealed.

The strident voice of Mrs Simpson cut across

whatever remark Jordan Kerr would have made in reply to Serena's defiant stand.

'Aren't we running a bit late, Jordan?' she demanded, unable to keep the irritation out of her voice at his preoccupation with Mrs Tonetti and her granddaughter.

His slight frown of displeasure showed that he had not liked the interruption, but he answered casually enough, giving Myrna a quick smile and brief salute in greeting as he said, 'It's all under control.'

Serena's hopes that he would now move on were quickly dashed as she saw him glance at his watch, then turn his attention back to her. 'I'll see you later,' he said softly but meaningly, and favoured Mrs Tonetti with another charming smile. 'It seems,' he drawled, 'that she needs a little more persuading. But I think we'll eventually convince her, don't you?'

Mrs Tonetti chuckled. 'Jordan, that sounded a little like a threat! Stop teasing her. Of course I want her to stay, but there are other considerations, you know—her job, for instance.'

His eyes rested momentarily on Serena before he replied laconically, 'Ah, yes, her job, of course.'

There was a deep gong-like sound and Jordan Kerr glanced again at his watch. 'Time I was moving,' he said casually, and with a brief salute went back the way he had come.

As she watched him stride away Serena knew she

hadn't as yet won the game; all she had accomplished was a brief stay of execution. That 'see you later', threat would take place at the ball that evening, she was sure. Her lips tightened; it couldn't come quick enough for her; the sooner he learnt you couldn't just push people around like that, the better! She had never thought she would be grateful for Roger's attention, not to mention protection. In fact, the more she thought about the coming interview, the more she found she was looking forward to it. She had been so shocked by Jordan Kerr's disclosures thrown at her as it were out of the blue, she had temporarily lost her senses. Now she had regained them and even that autocratic chunk of masculinity would be forced to see the sense of her argument.

She relaxed and smiled at Mrs Tonetti, who had been holding a conversation with a friend of hers who had just arrived, and was now able to give Serena her undivided attention.

'I must say,' she commented with twinkling eyes, 'Jordan seems to have taken an interest in you, Serena. Perhaps we won't have to look far for an excuse for you to stay after all.'

Serena's brows went up, feigning surprise; if only Mrs Tonetti knew just how near the mark she was! Only for entirely different reasons from the ones Serena guessed she was hoping for. 'Well, he does take your welfare to heart, doesn't he?' she replied airily, deliberately misconstruing the subtle hint.

Mrs Tonetti chuckled again, then said softly, 'Yes, he does, but I've an idea there's a little more to it this time.'

Serena was saved the necessity of thinking up a suitable rejoiner as a shout went up from the crowd on the beach. 'There she blows!'

Her breath caught in her throat as she looked ahead of her—there, just appearing from the screen of palms, was a full-masted galleon. It moved slowly but majestically into the bay—an awesome, yet wonderful sight. Serena sat entranced; she felt as if the years had rolled back. This, then, was how the first Kerr had come to the island to claim it for himself and his descendants. She wondered how the inhabitants had felt when they sighted the great ship. Her eyes fixed on the flag now plainly visible and a cold feeling played along her spine as she saw its markings. It was black with crossed swords worked in gold and somehow more daunting than the skull and crossbones motif.

The cold eyes and harsh voice of Jordan Kerr came unbidden to her as she watched the long boats being lowered slowly down the sides of the ship. Mrs Tonetti had said he was the image of the first Jordan Kerr, and Serena could well believe it! And not only in looks, she thought; this man would be just as ruthless in obtaining his objective, as she had good cause to know!

94

Making a mental effort to shrug off these thoughts, Serena asked Mrs Tonetti about the galleon. 'Is it the original one?' she queried.

'Yes, dear. Of course, it's had to be renovated from time to time, timbers replaced and so on, but it's been faithfully reproduced each time. It's kept in the blue lagoon, beyond the palms over there. There are some natural caves that provide an ideal shelter for it. It's quite an attraction for the tourists on its own.'

The first of the long boats was just heading into the beach, and Serena watched as its piratical occupants leapt out on to the shore uttering blood-curdling shouts and waving wicked-looking cutlasses. By the way the crowd scattered, accompanied by the shrieks from the ladies, one would almost think it was for real, Serena mused as she watched, then suddenly she stiffened. The leader of the first boat ashore was none other than Jordan Kerr; there was no mistaking his height and the way he carried himself. His hair touched by the rays of the sun was a fiery red and as she watched him he suddenly lifted his head and she felt as if he were looking straight at her.

Trying to still her racing pulses, she told herself she was imagining things again. Myrna was up there, wasn't she?

The shouting on the beach had now turned to laughter and squeals of mock terror, and Serena turned her attention there and half-smiled when she saw the reason. The pirates were capturing the girls of their choice, slinging them over their shoulders and making their way back to the boats. So that was why Jordan Kerr had been looking up there—he was warning Myrna!

When the awesome figure of the pirate captain hove into view, Serena felt no qualms but only wondered whether Myrna would put up a mild struggle or charmingly surrender.

As it turned out, Myrna had no choice, nor had Serena! Her eyes opened to full capacity as he stood before her and with a slight ironic bow said quite distinctly, 'My prize, I think.'

Before she could move Serena found herself flung over his shoulder and being borne off back down the incline to the beach. His hold was not gentle either —he might have been carrying a sack of potatoes, she thought furiously as she struggled to free herself. Her hat parted company from her as he landed on the beach. 'Put me down!' she hissed angrily. 'I've lost my hat and it's the only one I've got!'

It was as if he hadn't heard her, yet Serena was sure he had. 'Do you hear?' she demanded, making another frantic attempt to dislodge herself from his hold.

'I hear,' he said in a clipped tone. 'Someone will collect your hat. That's the least of your worries right now. You and I are going to have a little talk.'

'So we talk,' snapped Serena, vainly trying to keep her hair out of her eyes, but held as she was hanging over his shoulder it was no easy task. 'For your information, I'm not a yoga addict,' she added icily. 'Put me down, will you?'

'And worry Mrs Tonetti?' he said sarcastically. 'Oh, no; this is the way it's got to be done. Take it or leave it.'

Making a grab at her shoulder bag which was threatening to join the hat, she thought bitterly, as if she had any choice!

Serena's uncomfortable journey was over when they reached the boats and she was unceremoniously dumped in the nearest one. As she sat trying to get her breath back she looked up and met the amused eyes of a vaguely familiar pirate and when he spoke she placed him; it was Gerald. 'Seems I wasn't quick enough,' he said in a low voice, glancing at Jordan Kerr now busy organising the oarsmen for the return journey to the ship.

Following his glance, Serena saw Myrna Simpson, her pert straw still miraculously in position. Gerald, then, had 'captured' Myrna, and from the sulky expression on her face, Serena presumed Myrna had not liked that one bit. As if she felt her gaze on her, Myrna looked straight at her and Serena almost held her breath. It was a look of pure dislike, and Serena was sure she knew the reason for Jordan Kerr's interest in her. He would, of course, have had to make her promise to keep the information to herself. Not an easy task, Serena thought, particularly when it made someone like Myrna take a back seat for probably the first time in her life.

At a sharp order from Jordan Kerr, Gerald was pulled into service, obeying the order with a wry grin at Serena.

As the boat slowly put out to sea, Serena, watching the oarsmen, found her eyes inescapably drawn to Jordan Kerr. He led the stroke and his powerful shoulders bent forward and backward with the dip of the oars. She noticed that unlike the rest of the men he wore a peacock blue bandanna, and although his dress was of the same period as Jake's and the rest of the men, that was as far as the resemblance went. His shirt was of fine linen with lace cuffs that fell in soft folds against the tan of those strong hands of his. Serena wondered if it could be the original worn by his predecessor, and was almost certain the sleeveless jerkin of black velvet with gold threaded stitching in intricate patterns was indeed as old as it looked.

She glanced up as they neared the ship, then wished she hadn't as it loomed up in front of her like a gigantic whale. Surely they wouldn't be expected to scale that? But as they neared the side it became painfully obvious by the rope ladders hanging in wait that that was just what was expected of them. She glanced quickly at Myrna to find her watching

Jordan with a possessive glint in her eye. She didn't, thought Serena, look a bit perturbed at the prospect of scaling what appeared to Serena as the side of a mountain! Her glance then fell on Myrna's shoes; sensible navy blue pumps. Myrna would know the drill, of course. Serena then looked at her own footwear, surveying the slim platform soles with dismay; there was nothing there to give her grip. Well, she didn't know what the point was in hauling the girls to the ship, and they would have to return the same way they came anyway, so she would stay right where she was, ready for the return journey.

Unfortunately for Serena, Jordan Kerr had his own ideas on what she would do and made no bones about it. He was the first on the rope ladder and indicated briefly that she should follow. Serena stared at him, then at the swaying ladder, and went pale. She was hopeless at heights; she gave a decisive shake of the head. 'I'll wait for the return journey,' she announced firmly.

'You'll only get wet if you fall,' drawled Myrna behind her.

'My weight holds the ladder firm,' said Jordan Kerr in the sort of voice that told Serena she was going up that ladder whether she liked it or not.

'I'm right behind you, Serena,' Gerald offered encouragingly.

'I still think I'll stay,' said Serena, making a last-ditch stand, and remembering her shoes held one foot slightly in the air. 'I couldn't possibly get a grip in these, could I?' she appealed to Gerald, who she felt she could rely on to protect her interests.

Jordan Kerr's eyes narrowed and he gave her another ironic half bow. 'You have been snatched by pirates, milady, and therefore have no choice.'

About to argue the point, Serena for the second time that day found herself hauled up and over Jordan Kerr's shoulder. While marvelling at his strength for he had still kept one hand on the ladder, she rather felt things had gone far enough and kicked out in an attempt to dislodge his hold. She wasn't afraid of falling in the water; anything was preferable to this sort of treatment.

Myrna gave a derisive, 'Really! I know we're supposed to be entertaining the visitors, but there's no need to overdo it. For goodness' sake, Jordan, if she's so scared, leave her. We'll not be staying long anyway.'

Gerald heartily agreed with this sentiment. 'It's the height, I expect, old boy. And she's not like the rest of the girls, they knew what was coming.'

Neither need have spoken, for Jordan Kerr had started the ascent with a hold of iron against Serena's kicking legs and useless protests.

'I say,' began Gerald indignantly, 'aren't you carrying ...'

'You look after your catch and I'll look after mine,' Jordan Kerr interjected, adding smoothly,

'All's fair in love and war.'

Serena closed her eyes—and this was war, there was no doubt about it! Her face brushed the smooth velvet of his jacket and felt the slight roughness of the worked-in stitching. It was a lie, she thought hysterically, that first piratical character that took the island hadn't died at all! He was still here; just as ruthless as he had been all those years ago!

CHAPTER SEVEN

ONCE they were on deck Serena found herself put down with the same carelessness as she had been dumped in the boat. With an abrupt, 'Follow me,' Jordan Kerr went on ahead with Serena languidly following.

To ease her frustration at such treatment Serena worked out ways as to how she could make this ruthless character pay for her humiliation. An apology simply wouldn't be good enough, she thought. Not even if he went down on his knees! Almost tripping over a heavy rope, she decided she would sue him. He was a very rich man, wasn't he?—well, she wouldn't have to worry about her mother's expenditure in future; in fact she would encourage it! It would be Jordan Kerr's money they would be spending!

The uneven deck made her stumble suddenly and as her shoulder-bag swung open, scattering most of its contents on to the deck, she cast a look of fury at the tall form striding in front of her. As she stooped to pick them up, her fingers were just too late in reaching her passport. One large brown hand was there before her.

Giving Jordan Kerr a look of pure dislike, she

held out her hand for the passport. 'Thank you,' she murmured coldly.

To her further fury he calmly ignored her outstretched hand and placed it in his jerkin pocket, then without a word walked on in front of her again.

Wanting to scream at him but knowing it wouldn't get her anywhere, Serena was forced to follow him. She almost stopped in her tracks as a thought hit her—her passport! Why, oh, why hadn't she thought of that before—you couldn't manufacture passports! Her name was on it— just let him argue that one away!

Precisely two minutes later that was exactly what he did do! Seated in what she presumed was the captain's quarters, Serena listened while her brainwave went up in smoke.

'I have to hand it to you,' he drawled. 'On anyone else, it might have worked. Unfortunately, I know a little too much about you. When I said I'd given up the search for you, it wasn't strictly true. I just passed the odious task on to a highly reputable detective agency. I know for a fact that you have two aliases, so why not a third? The sort of company you kept you'd know how to get your hand on a passport. That information is now paying off, isn't it?—but not to your advantage, I'm afraid.'

Serena's glimpse into the wily ways of the underworld was something of a revelation to her. However, she felt she could have done without it at this particular time. She was now getting slightly desperate. 'Look!' she began, forcing herself to remain calm, knowing it was imperative that she somehow got through to him. 'Can't you see it would be better for me to go? I promise to write to Mrs Tonetti and keep in touch.'

'You can't even call her Grandmother, can you?' he said harshly. 'As for keeping in touch, I don't believe a word of it. Once back to the bright lights and you'll conveniently forget she exists.' His eyes narrowed. 'There's nothing for you to come back for, is there? There's nothing left for you to inherit, you really shouldn't have been quite so greedy before.'

Serena's eyes flashed; she wanted to hit out at him, but knew he was having trouble keeping his hands off her and would dearly love an excuse to throttle her, so provoking him would not help. 'All right!' she said bitterly. 'I only wanted to explain the position—and believe it or not prevent Mrs Tonetti from ...' she faltered a little on seeing the tigerish flash her constant use of the name produced, then went on firmly, knowing it was no use trying to convince him she wasn't Lisa Tonetti. 'How will it look,' she demanded, 'when the man I'm practically engaged to charges in on the next plane? You won't be able to bully him, I can assure you; and Roger knows nothing about Mrs Tonetti,' she paused, biting her lip. 'For goodness' sake! Can't you see the result? How can I explain a grandmother he never knew existed—let alone explain that I've decided to stay with her? If you think Roger will leave it at that, you're very much mistaken. He won't rest until he knows the whole story, and that you're keeping me on the island by force. Just how are you going to explain that part of it to my—er—grandmother?'

Seeing the start he gave at her last question, Serena felt a surge of triumph. He couldn't argue against that—not if he wanted to protect Mrs Tonetti. She pressed on with her advantage. 'Short of kidnapping Roger at the airport,' she purred, 'there's nothing you can do about it. Roger,' she said sweetly, 'will not take kindly to being pushed around. He also has business connections,' she added airily, feeling as if a great weight had been lifted off her shoulders. 'I'm quite sure he can match whatever influence you think you have in certain circles.' She flashed him a smile of triumph. 'So in the circumstances I think you'll agree it would be better if I went, don't you?'

Noticing the small muscle twitch at the side of Jordan Kerr's mouth, Serena felt like cheering. He was furious and she could feel the inward struggle he was having not to shake the daylights out of her. She had him cornered; not a position he was used to; she doubted whether such a thing had ever happened before to him. Her relief that it was all over made her magnanimous. 'I meant what I said about keeping in touch with my—grandmother,' she added kindly.

Completely ignoring her last remark, Jordan Kerr shot out, 'Roger who?'

Serena almost grinned; he had chosen not to believe her again. A few inquiries would ascertain Roger's existence and his standing in the business world, not to mention the fact that Serena Belmont was a person in her own right and not an alias.

'Roger Alton,' she replied, her eyes squarely meeting the ice flecked ones carefully watching her.

His brows rose sardonically. 'You do fly high, don't you?' he commented sarcastically. 'I suppose the poor devil's well and truly hooked.'

An indignant Serena felt a start of surprise that he had heard of Roger, and she chose to ignore his other comments. She would make an extra fuss of Roger, she thought, when she saw him on Saturday, and she even felt it possible to forgive his encouraging her mother. As for this domineering character ... 'I can't say it's been nice meeting you,' she snapped as she got up to leave and held her hand out for her passport. 'My passport, if you please.'

'But I don't please,' he said in a soft deadly voice. 'You very nearly brought it off, didn't you? I'm going to take a leaf out of your book. You've had a change of heart, Miss Tonetti—we're engaged,' he said, smiling unpleasantly at Serena's white face and wide eyes echoing the shock his words had produced.

He nodded grimly. 'Yes, I would go that far to

make you pay your debt to your grandmother. I'm not so easily discouraged as you'll soon find out. So your friend arrives breathing fire and brimstone—let him! There's not much he can do about it, is there? It's happening all the time, isn't it?' he said casually.

Somehow Serena found her voice. 'You're mad!' she said huskily. 'Roger will never believe a story like that.' She shook her head as if to dispel the cotton wool feeling of unreality. 'For goodness' sake,' she said wearily, 'if you haven't a better card to play than that, I should forget it—it won't work. Why not for once accept defeat? In spite of what you think I am not Lisa Tonetti and I do intend to leave on Saturday.'

He leaned back in his chair and folding his arms across his powerful chest surveyed her through narrowed eyes. 'Oh, but he will,' he said silkily. 'Especially when a few unpleasant facts come to light. I'm considered a good catch, you know, and can more than match him in the financial stakes.'

Serena wondered whether it was her imagination or not, but the captain's quarters seemed to be getting smaller and the man sitting in front of her, larger. Her eyes flicked nervously towards him as he sat calmly watching her much as a cat watched a mouse it had trapped. She felt the cold feeling run down her spine and managed to suppress a shiver. He would enjoy watching her quake. With a mental effort she pulled herself together, that diabolical costume he wore hardly helped either, but she wasn't going to be intimidated by that.

'Why do you hate her so much?' she asked suddenly.

Jordan's face had a closed look about it as he answered coldly, 'Hate? Oh, no; hate is an emotion, Miss Tonetti, and where you're concerned I have no emotions. A motive, yes; to make you pay for the misery you caused your grandparents.' His eyes met hers inexorably. 'So why don't you take your own advice and give in gracefully?' He grinned satanically. 'I can well understand your refusal to acknowledge your name; it's a well known psychological fact that the mind rejects what it doesn't want to remember. I do realise how hard it must be for you particularly as it appears you've now turned—er—respectable.' He gave her a glinting look. 'Not only respectable,' he went on smoothly, 'but with a rosy future in front of you as the wife of a successful financier.' He shook his head mockingly. 'It couldn't have happened at a worse time, could it? Being found out, I mean. You have my deepest sympathy.'

'Sympathy!' echoed Serena, almost choking over the word. 'You don't know the meaning of the word!'

Unable to bear another minute in his presence, she got up quickly and turned towards the cabin door, but he was there before her, covering the distance between them in seconds. Serena could hardly credit that a man of his size could move so swiftly.

He held her arm in a painful grip. 'Oh, no, you don't,' he bit out. 'Is this the way to behave with your beloved?' he jeered. 'Remember, my sweet, it was love at first sight.'

His eyes narrowed as he traced the delicate lines of her features. 'A great pity,' he murmured. 'You look so innocent too. You really are one of the devil's angels, aren't you?'

Serena could feel the magnetism of the man who stood so close beside her. He was so tall he had to bend his head to avoid contact with the low oak rafters, bringing his face dangerously close to hers. Her eyes fell on the well-moulded lips and she wondered what his kiss was like, then blushed as she realised where these thoughts were leading her.

'So we can still blush, can we?' he said hatefully. 'Or is it temper? Of course, it must be. You're way beyond the blushing stage, aren't you?'

Serena tried to break the compelling hold he had on her arm, but he only tightened his hold. She winced as the steel-like fingers bit into her arm. It appeared she had lost hands down, nothing she could say would convince Jordan Kerr he had made a mistake and yet she had to try, Roger was not a fool and not likely to be taken in by the ridiculous story of an engagement to someone she barely knew. She ignored his taunts and the temptation to slap that arrogant face; she was in enough trouble without asking for more. Managing to keep her voice calm, she said, 'I still say you'll have to think again. An engagement after only two days is hardly feasible, is it?' She swallowed. 'Roger mustn't come here,' she added quickly. 'You must see that.'

This produced his grim smile again and his hand relaxed his hold on her arm. Serena quickly drew away from him. 'Most perceptive of you,' he sneered. 'Only it's a little longer than two days, isn't it?' he went on silkily. 'You arrived on Saturday, didn't you?' He acknowledged her start grimly. 'I've done a little checking, you see. Oh, you kept well away from the other guests, and it's not hard to guess why. There was no point in advertising your presence before you'd done a little research and found out if it was really worth your while to attempt a reconciliation. What had you in mind? A touch for the trousseau outlay? They had been very generous in the past, hadn't they?'

Serena's fingers clenched; she was finding it hard to believe that anyone could be as bad as Jordan Kerr was painting Lisa Tonetti. It appeared to be a fixation of his and his vehemence didn't really justify the cause. So he was protecting Mrs Tonetti because he was fond of her—or was there a little more to it? Serena was sure there was.

Jordan Kerr's smooth voice cut into her musings. 'Going back to your Roger I find myself for once in agreement with you, for very different reasons, of course. Mine being the welfare of a very old friend; yours—self-preservation.' His eyes narrowed. 'You're very sure of him at the moment, aren't you? And I'm pretty certain you don't give a damn about the man himself; it's what he can give you that matters, isn't it?'

Serena flushed. He meant that she didn't love Roger, and she didn't, but she couldn't very well argue that one through.

Watching her reaction he nodded, grimly satisfied. 'Very smart of you not to attempt to deny it. It seems you do give me credit for not being stupid enough to believe otherwise.'

He was silent for a few seconds and Serena hoped that she had managed to persuade him to let her go. The door was so close, yet so far, she knew if she made a move towards it she would receive that painful hold again. He hadn't finished with her yet.

'I'll have the airport watched,' he said abruptly. 'If Alton comes, as I presume he will, we face him together.'

'T—together ...?' faltered Serena.

Jordan Kerr gave her a look of distaste. 'Together,' he confirmed. 'We can hardly expect him to accept the story without your presence, can we?'

Serena felt as if she were in a fast-moving river and slowly going under. If Roger came, that would be that; she wasn't that good an actress and the whole charade would be exposed. She shook her head vehemently. 'No!' she exclaimed. 'It won't do.'

Jordan Kerr studied her insolently. 'It must,' he sneered. 'And don't work out any schemes for evading the issue, either. But then you're smart, aren't you? No doubt you've already worked out the penalty for failure. Not only will you lose the chance of a rich husband—if things work out for you, that is, but you'll find yourself on the wanted list. I shall immediately press charges against you. When it's over ...' his face hardened and Serena knew he was referring to Mrs Tonetti's death, 'you can patch things up with him always providing he hasn't found anyone else, he doesn't sound too fussy, at that. So you might consider you're getting off lightly when you stop to think about it. A few months of what you'll probably consider hard labour after the kind of life you've been leading, at the beck and call of your grandmother, and I'll be around often enough to see you keep to the bargain.

'Nothing more,' he added disdainfully, 'will be required of you, and don't start getting ideas of staying on and capitalizing on our association, will you? When the time comes I want you off my land. You'll be pushed on to the first plane to touch down. Alton's welcome to you.'

CHAPTER EIGHT

FOR the rest of that day Jordan Kerr was Serena's constant companion. The only breathing space she was given came when she accompanied Mrs Tonetti back to the chalet to dress for the ball later that evening, and by that time the whole of the island must have been aware of Jordan Kerr's single-minded preference for Serena's company.

It was not easy for her to accept the role so unceremoniously thrown at her and on one or two occasions she was tersely directed to look as if she were enjoying herself, as he caustically pointed out in a low undertone, 'There's no pot of gold on the end of this rainbow; but think of the penalty you'll incur if you fail.'

Nor was it easy trying to meet Mrs Tonetti's twinkling eyes with an answering smile in hers, and it was taken for granted Serena would be staying longer than the original period. Apart from a knowing smile and an 'I told you so' look, nothing was said.

Quite apart from the problem of Roger's appearance on the island, Serena had her mother to consider, and both as yet were unaware of the fact that she would not be on the Saturday flight. All chance of slipping away to catch the flight was now lost; Jordan Kerr held her passport and was not likely to give it back to her until his conditions were fulfilled.

To save her mother worry Serena cabled her hotel telling her she would not be arriving Saturday, adding 'letter following'. Not that the letter would ever be written; it wouldn't be necessary—not after Roger was acquainted with the news!

Serena's spirits were low as she selected the dress she would wear for the ball, and as she slipped the frothy white organdie gown on she recalled Jordan Kerr's scathing remarks on her being one of the devil's angels. Her soft mouth twisted as she met her reflection in the dressing table mirror. If she remembered rightly, the gown had been christened 'temptation' by its aspiring creator. Not, she thought, as her eyes traced the clinging top and billowing skirt, that Jordan Kerr would be 'tempted'. Despite all outward appearance of his attentiveness, he had adroitly managed to keep his distance as far as physical contact was concerned, and Serena, recalling the painful hold he had clamped on her on the ship, was devoutly grateful for this small mercy; she was also grateful for the fact that the 'engagement' plan had not been put into operation, although she knew it was only held in abeyance to be used as and when necessary to ward Roger off.

As she picked up her evening bag, Serena tried to

imagine herself gazing up into Jordan Kerr's face with the adoration and love that would be required to convince Roger that she had fallen hopelessly in love with the masterful owner of the island, but found her imagination didn't stretch that far! It might have helped if she had liked the man, but she heartily disliked him. Quite apart from the rough treatment he had meted out to her, she was sure she wouldn't have liked him anyway, even if they had met in different circumstances. He was too sure of himself and too used to getting his own way. No middle way for such as he, she thought bitterly. There was but one way, Jordan Kerr's way; right or wrong, and in her case—wrong.

Serena was half-way to the lounge to join Mrs Tonetti when the thought hit her making her stop suddenly in her tracks. The engagement! She frowned; really, her wits must have gone begging! Once it was announced Mrs Tonetti would have to confess to Jordan Kerr that Serena was not her granddaughter! He hadn't believed Serena, but he would have to believe Mrs Tonetti! Her thoughts whirled on; as much as she dreaded Roger's arrival his appearance now was her only salvation.

Her frown deepened as she thought of the humiliation Mrs Tonetti would suffer should her deception ever get to Mrs Simpson's ears, then she relaxed slightly; Jordan Kerr might not care what happened to her, but he did care for Mrs Tonetti; he would keep the information to himself—and Myrna? Serena's eyes narrowed speculatively; she hadn't been sure before but she was now. Myrna knew nothing—she couldn't do! The knowledge gave her a little shock and for a moment her attitude towards Jordan Kerr softened, then her lips firmed. He was not a fool; knowledge like that in the hands of a jealous woman was pure dynamite! He wouldn't risk it and remembering Myrna's vicious glances in her direction, Serena heartily agreed with him.

Her step was a little lighter as she joined Mrs Tonetti in the lounge and noticing her pallor commented, 'Don't you think you ought to give this evening a miss? I'm sure Jordan will understand.'

Mrs Tonetti smiled. 'It's only excitement, dear,' she said. 'So tiring when you get old, you know.' She glanced down at her finely veined hands that trembled a little in her lap. 'Perhaps it would be wiser to stay and rest. However, I shall only do so on your promise that you attend—not,' she added mischievously, 'that Jordan will hear of you doing anything else.'

Serena smiled at her. 'You have my word,' she promised, then she fetched a footstool and placed it under Mrs Tonetti's feet. 'I'll just tell Molly you're staying,' she said, and walked to the door.

'No, dear, not just yet. I want to talk to you; you can tell Molly just before you leave.'

There was something about Mrs Tonetti's expression as she made this request that alerted Serena. Had she decided to tell Jordan the truth? Serena's hopes soared—she would catch that plane after all!

'Come and sit down, dear,' coaxed Mrs Tonetti in the sort of voice that suggested that she had bad news for her, and Serena wondered whether she had thought Jordan would lose interest in her once he knew the truth and was preparing her for it.

'I want to tell you about Jordan,' the old lady began hesitantly. Serena could have cheered; she had decided to confess! However, it soon became apparent that no such thought had entered her mind. A very deflated Serena listened to what Mrs Tonetti was telling her. 'Don't get too fond of him, dear,' she said slowly. 'Not at least until you're sure, that is. You see, I know him very well, and although he doesn't deliberately set out to hurt anyone, I'm afraid it's quite possible it might happen to you.' She sighed. 'Not that I've any sympathy for the others; as a very wealthy man he's a target for the fortune-hunters,' she lifted her hands expressively. 'And there's no denying he's a very good-looking man,' she half-smiled at this comment. 'I'm not too old to appreciate that,' she murmured, then sighed again. 'It's very sad, but I don't think he's ever stopped loving Maria. They were almost engaged, you know, and she died. She was only nineteen and the loveliest thing you ever saw—blonde, with huge baby-blue eyes.' Her voice softened as she spoke of the girl and Serena sensed that she had been very fond of her.

In spite of herself Serena was interested. 'How did she die?' she asked quietly.

Mrs Tonetti started as if she had been brought back from her memories as indeed she had. 'Drowned, dear.' She frowned. 'No one knows why she was swimming in that particular spot. It was a well-known danger zone, the currents are treacherous, and Maria should have known it was dangerous; she had been coming to the island for years. Her parents were close friends of Jordan's parents and although they lived in New York they were always here for weekends.' Once again she lapsed into reverie and Serena wanted to hear more, so she gently prompted her.

'How long ago did this happen, Mrs Tonetti?' she asked.

Mrs Tonetti frowned and concentrated on the question. 'Seven years, I think,' she answered musingly, and looked at Serena sadly. 'He's never bothered since to really look at any woman, not in that light, I mean. Oh, he flirts with them, of course, he's human after all, but they're just ships that pass in the night as far as he's concerned. You know, sometimes I wonder if he resents them because they are living and his love's dead.' She shook her head slowly. 'So you see, my dear, why you must be on your guard. He wouldn't deliberately set out to hurt you, he wouldn't see that you're not like the others, and the fact that he thinks you're my granddaughter wouldn't make the slightest difference either, I'm afraid. So do be careful, Serena. Hold on to your heart until you're certain he's not just having a fling with you.'

There was not the slightest danger of Serena being in any such predicament, but she appreciated Mrs Tonetti's confidential advice. For one thing it explained why his persecution of her amounted to a vendetta! Serena's fingers clenched into a fist. She couldn't wait for Roger's arrival and to be able to tell Jordan Kerr just what she thought of him!

The cablegram came just as Serena was leaving. It was from her mother and just stated that she would be arriving at noon the following day. Serena pushed the message quickly into her bag, and hoped Mrs Tonetti, who had gone to bed earlier, had not seen the messenger arrive. It was just another complication for Serena to deal with. For goodness' sake—why her mother and not Roger? She simply couldn't see Roger allowing her mother to chase after her; he would consider it *his* duty.

Stepping out on to the tiled porchway of the chalet, Serena watched the Rolls glide to a graceful halt beside her and her spirits sank as she saw who had collected her. He didn't even bother to get out but leaned over and opened the door for her, even

Jake, she thought scathingly, had more manners than his autocratic employer.

As she sat stiffly beside him she felt the slight rustle of the paper under her fingers. Well, there was no time like the present, she thought. 'My mother's arriving tomorrow,' she announced airily. 'Try convincing her I'm Lisa Tonetti!'

He thrust her a glinting look. 'Boy-friend backed out?' he asked with grim amusement. 'Your mother died six years ago,' he said harshly. 'I can even tell you how; in a car crash after having imbibed a little too much of her favourite beverage. Now this—er—mother,' he said musingly, 'she'd be genteelly bred, of course, down on her luck, probably through gambling losses and just right for your proposition. Of course, it wouldn't work unless you had some sort of family, would it? You needed a respectable background—could be tricky on your own home ground, though, so she probably resides elsewhere, called in as it were when necessary. It's been worked before, of course, quite successfully too. When the fish is landed there's a share-out and little monthly payments, not too much, but just enough to keep the bogus parent happy.' He gave the stunned Serena another glinting look. 'You didn't really think I'd fall for that, did you?'

It occurred to Serena that if she ever did break free from Jordan Kerr's pernicious hold, she might well take to a life of crime; it would be a pity to waste the first-class training she was receiving! Answering his last taunt, she said abruptly, 'No, Mr Kerr, I can't say I can see you falling for anything, particularly when it doesn't suit your convenience. You've got it all taped, haven't you? I must say I'm a little intrigued over what sort of an apology you'll give after meeting my mother. After the treatment I've received, it had better be a good one,' she muttered darkly.

As he swung the car into his drive, he answered casually, 'As it's such an unlikely event, I shouldn't worry your head about it. Why didn't you mention this mother of yours before? It's a little late to bring that tactic into play, isn't it? Or is she likely to make trouble if she thinks you're running out on her?'

Serena did not answer simply because what he had said was partially true—she ought to have told him about her mother; it might have helped earlier—now it was too late. She now wished she had never mentioned her, for she could have arranged to slip out and meet that plane and apprise her of the facts. It was a situation that would appeal to her immensely, and Serena knew she could rely on her to come up with some story to fob off a visit from Roger in the near future. Serena sighed. She always seemed to think of these things afterwards. If Jordan Kerr hadn't had such a chip on his shoulder he might have seen that she wasn't half so bright as he credited Lisa Tonetti with being.

The car slithered to a halt outside the house and Jordan got out. Serena, not waiting to be assisted, also got out and walked towards the steps to the house. To her intense irritation he placed a hand on her arm in what could hardly be called a lover-like hold and she shrugged it off furiously.

Giving a low laugh, he then placed an arm around her slender waist and clamped her to his side. It was a hold Serena couldn't break and she knew this was only the start of the evening. 'Must you be so brutal?' she said in a low voice. 'It doesn't help, does it?'

'It's the only way I can stomach the whole business,' he replied curtly. 'I haven't your experience in double-dealing. I must say I'm a little disappointed in you,' his eyes held hers mockingly. 'You're passing up a golden opportunity. I'm rich and fancy free.' His hand increased its pressure and Serena winced. 'You never know,' he said silkily, 'there just might be something in it for you.'

Serena had a cold feeling again—he was challenging her, and she only wished she had the courage to take him up on it, for she could make things very unpleasant for him as she recalled his barely disguised distaste of her nearness when she had danced with him the previous evening. Her eyes sparkled; she would do it! This time the idea hadn't come too late! She would positively drool over him! He had wanted to create the impression that they were in love, hadn't he? And there was absolutely nothing he could do about it while they were in company. Afterwards ... Serena decided she wouldn't dwell too much on that part of it. No matter what happened it would be worth it!

CHAPTER NINE

LONG afterwards, Serena wondered how she had found the courage to carry out her plan of discomfiting Jordan Kerr, for it was one thing telling herself she would do so, quite another carrying it out!

She did not attempt to bring the tactic into play until they were in full view of the assembly, then she shamelessly clung to his arm and almost chuckled at the start he gave. With no little satisfaction she watched his jaw harden and a glint appear in his eyes that promised retribution at no late date; but Serena refused to be intimidated.

As his arm pinned hers to his side he murmured in a low undertone, 'There's no need to overdo it. I abhor clinging women.'

Smiling at one of the guests standing a little way beyond them, Serena replied sweetly, 'I'm only following your advice. Stupid of me to waste such a golden opportunity. Remember, Jordan, darling, I know all the tricks.'

She knew by the indrawn breath that she had infuriated him and there was simply nothing he could do about it.

Myrna and her partner, a Mr Canning, an elderly retired colonel, left the dance floor and joined Mrs

Simpson just as Serena and Jordan approached. Myrna was looking particularly stunning in an apricot velvet off-the-shoulder gown that highlighted her fair colouring, and it occurred to Serena that she might well have reminded Jordan of his lost Maria. Men, she mused, were apt to be attracted by one particular type of woman—not, she thought, looking at Myrna's cold blue eyes, that anyone in their right mind could call her eyes baby blue, more like ice blue, she thought, as they rested on her for a brief second.

Completely ignoring Serena, Myrna placed a proprietorial hand on Jordan's free arm and gazed up at him coquettishly. 'I absolutely demand the next dance, darling,' she murmured throatily to him.

Serena almost felt sorry for Jordan. He must have longed to accept the invitation so seductively offered, but could hardly do so with Serena clinging to his other arm. Taking pity on him, she removed her arm and giving him what she hoped was a brilliant smile murmured with the same throaty intonation as Myrna, 'Do go ahead; I've no right to monopolise your company.'

Having seen Gerald approaching, Serena was confident she would at least be able to enjoy one dance and smiled at him as he joined them. To her fury Jordan decided the matter by firmly taking her arm and smiling half apologetically at Myrna, suggested,

'Later, perhaps?' and led Serena on to the dance floor.

While she waited for Jordan to take her hand and place his arm round her waist for the opening steps of the dreamy music Serena consoled herself that he was not likely to ask her to dance again—she would see to that.

As before, his clasp on her hand was light, and she had no difficulty in disengaging it and placing it on his shoulder to enable her to move closer to him; a move she had seen carried out by her more un-inhibited friends and one Serena would never have dared to imitate not even if she had felt attracted to the man in question—and when the man was Jordan Kerr ... She felt him stiffen and knew he was ap-palled at the bold move. Again, there was nothing he could do about it; they were in full view of the whole room and any attempt to thrust her away from him would not fail to be seen.

His free arm now had to go round Serena, com-pletely enclosing her, and she winced as he jerked her closer and made herself go pliant in his arms.

His voice was harsh as he spoke close to her hair. 'Is this part of the softening-up process? Pity it's go-ing to be wasted, isn't it?' he jeered softly as he swung her round swiftly so that she was jerked against his hard lean body in quick succession.

When Serena had partially recovered her breath she threw caution to the wind and muttered, 'Just try and get me to dance with you again—I'd rather go to jail!'

His answer was a low chuckle. 'Nice to know you're enjoying it as much as I am, but you asked for it.'

Miserably Serena had to acknowledge the truth of this, but for once Jordan Kerr was as uncomfortable as she was, and that fact alone gave her some consolation.

However, it did serve to achieve her aim, for although the band immediately struck up another melody, Jordan did not request an encore but suggested they seek refreshment, a suggestion Serena was only too happy to agree with. Her waist felt as if it had just been released from an iron band and she wondered if the bruises would show later.

If Jordan was hoping for a short respite from the outward appearance of dancing attendance on her, he was doomed to disappointment, as the first people they encountered as they entered the supper room were no other than Mrs Simpson and a friend of hers. Mrs Simpson immediately pounced on him.

'Jordan! Margaret has just told me she hasn't seen the portrait of the first Jordan Kerr. I was just telling her of the likeness. Do you think we could go and see it now?'

Sensing that it was a move on Mrs Simpson's part to detach her from his side, Serena was all for it; she was almost sure he would accompany the ladies and not waiting to hear his answer walked towards the buffet in search of a long cold drink.

'Serena?'

To her extreme annoyance Serena found him beside her before she had swallowed a mouthful of her drink.

'I'm sure you'll find the portrait interesting,' he said smoothly, not giving her a chance of refusing. 'Shall we go?'

Putting down the drink, Serena forced herself to sound interested. 'Of course,' she said airily, meeting Mrs Simpson's snapping black eyes.

'We're honoured, you know,' Mrs Simpson commented casually. 'Myrna's the only one so far to be given a private viewing.'

Serena wondered if she felt better after having got that broadside in.

Staring at the life-size painting a few minutes later, Serena had to steel herself to suppress a shiver as she gazed at the cold eyes of the man in the portrait—and not only in front of her, she thought nervily, but at the side of her as well. The likeness was uncanny, the only physical difference being in the colour of the eyes. The pirate's were a dark blue, whereas Jordan Kerr's were that curious light green. It was hard to believe that the man she was looking at had lived centuries ago, yet the man whose eyes she could feel boring into her and standing by her side dressed immaculately in a dark tuxedo could have stepped straight out of the picture.

Her thoughts were echoed by Margaret, who exclaimed, 'It's uncanny, isn't it?' in an awed voice.

Serena knew Jordan's eyes were still on her as he answered casually, 'I believe the resemblance is there in more ways than one.'

'What nonsense, Jordan!' simpered Mrs Simpson. 'From what I hear of the island's history that gentleman gave no quarter. Of course,' she added magnanimously, 'things were different in those days. He had to be hard to survive.'

'Precisely,' murmured Jordan, and again Serena sensed his eyes on her. 'Given the same circumstances, I, too, would give no quarter.' He dismissed Mrs Simpson's eager attempt to refute this sweeping statement with a careless wave of the hand towards the portrait. 'Believe me, my ancestor and I have a lot in common. Now, shall we join the other guests?'

After this little interlude it was doubly hard for Serena to revert back to the clinging stage with Jordan. Her every instinct cautioned her to keep her distance; she knew his words had been for her alone, a veiled warning to her not to cross him.

Ushering Mrs Simpson and her friend out of the library, he mockingly held his arm out for Serena's hand and she was forced to accept it, but he did not miss her reluctance, and as they followed the others back to the ballroom he inquired softly, 'Lost your enthusiasm? I would have thought my worthy ancestor would have suited you admirably—in a way he had a lot in common with you, he took what he wanted, too.'

'Yet you persecute me and glorify him,' Serena grated back in a low voice. 'How many lives did he take in getting what he wanted? I would rather my conscience than his!'

She found herself swung round to face him. He held her in a biting grip close to him and had either of the two ladies in front chanced to turn round at that precise time, they would have gained the impression that Jordan was kissing her. However, no such thought was in his mind as he surveyed her through hooded lids. When he spoke his voice was harsh.

'What he took, he took fair and square. Fought for it. He didn't wait until the coast was clear and sneak in the back way, nor,' he added scathingly, 'did he rob his friends.'

He released her abruptly and Serena turned away from him quickly. There was nothing she could say to that—nothing he would believe anyway, she thought dully.

As she wearily prepared for bed later that evening, Serena's thoughts were centred on her mother and her proposed visit the next day. As no further mention of the subject had been made by Jordan Kerr, she presumed he had dismissed it as a story she had thought up to gain her freedom. It looked as if it was the first piece of luck she had had for some time, and she was determined not to make a hash of it. Her mother must be told of the bizarre situation she had landed herself in and go back to New York by the next plane if necessary, and apprise Roger of the facts. He could then come armed with all the necessary information to outflank Jordan Kerr. Serena, banging her pillows into a more comfortable shape, dwelt on this happening with relish. Why, she would be so grateful to Roger she might even consider marrying him!

Her brow creased as she thought of Mrs Tonetti. An excuse would have to be found to cover her absence. She would say she had some shopping to do—of course, she could tell her the truth, but on thinking it over, Serena decided against this. It might worry the old lady, and she might feel duty bound to invite her mother to the chalet and that would mean all sorts of complications. Serena felt the situation was complicated enough without adding more!

During her solitary breakfast the following morning, she rehearsed in her mind what she would tell her mother. There wouldn't be time to go into details. Roger had to be made to understand that his visit concerned only Jordan Kerr, and no one else, and that the information Mrs Belmont gave him should remain strictly private.

Having got everything clear in her mind, Serena was able to greet Mrs Tonetti with a bright smile when she joined her later and answer her query as to whether she had enjoyed herself the previous evening and whether Jordan had brought her back.

Serena knew Mrs Tonetti was trying to gauge just how interested Jordan Kerr was in her and felt it wise to play it down. In the not too distant future the 'interest' would be non-existent and Serena would be sunning herself on the deck of a luxury yacht and wondering why she had allowed herself to be pushed around by a modern version of Long John Silver!

Her musings were interrupted by the appearance of Molly, who told her she was wanted on the telephone. Feeling a stab of apprehension, Serena went to take the call. Had her mother taken an earlier flight? Giving a cautious 'hallo', she was half relieved to hear the deep voice of Jordan on the other end of the line—relieved, that was, until she heard the reason for the call.

'I'm picking you up at eleven-forty-five,' he said curtly.

Serena did a double-take; whatever happened she didn't want Jordan Kerr around today of all days. 'I've decided to spend the day with my grandmother,' she said sweetly. 'Tomorrow, perhaps?'

'Liar,' he said softly. 'You didn't think I'd forgotten your—er—mother's arrival, did you? Eleven-forty-five,' he repeated slowly, and put the phone down on her.

'Jordan has other plans, I take it?' said Mrs Tonetti behind her.

Serena forced herself to sound gay—not easy when she wanted to shout and rave, either that, or howl her eyes out, but she was even denied this luxury. 'I'm afraid so,' she managed to say with a weak smile. 'He's calling later.'

Mrs Tonetti nodded happily. 'I thought so,' she smiled.

Serena looked at her as she settled herself in her chair. If only ... 'Mrs Tonetti—Nan,' she began quickly. 'Oughtn't you to tell him?' she pleaded gently. 'It makes me feel such a fraud.'

Smiling fondly at her, Mrs Tonetti replied softly, 'If he loves you, dear. It won't make the slightest difference, you know.' Her smile faded and a frown creased her finely lined forehead. 'It's just that I'm not entirely convinced ...' She was silent for a moment as if weighing the matter up, then she looked up suddenly to find Serena worriedly watching her and smiled at her. 'I promise to tell him should it become necessary—don't look so worried, dear.' The faded blue eyes now held the pleading look. 'In my own way, Serena. It's not going to be easy, but if it's making you unhappy ...'

'No,' Serena replied hastily. 'It's not that, it's just that I felt he ought to be put in the picture.' She managed to bring a light note into the conversation.

'As you say, there's time enough for that if things get out of hand—and I can assure you,' she added firmly in order to take that anxious look away from Mrs Tonetti's expression, 'that I'm still heart-free and likely to remain so. Your Jordan is a bit too dominant for my liking. I much prefer the easy-to-manage types, saves a lot of arguing in the long run, you know.'

Watching Mrs Tonetti's frown replaced by her delightful smile, Serena breathed a sigh of relief. She might be in trouble, but it was infinitely preferable for things to remain as they were than to cause her kind hostess further misery.

Serena watched the plane touch down with mixed feelings. It was now up to her mother; she was very conscious of Jordan Kerr's grip on her arm in case she made a bolt for it or attempted to forewarn what he thought was her accomplice.

As the passengers streamed down the gangway, Serena had no difficulty in picking out her mother. Her ridiculously flimsy hat with layers of chiffon would not have looked out of place at Ascot, come to that, nor would her dress of shantung silk, Serena thought, and in spite of her anxiety she felt a spurt of pride. Who else but her mother would have dared to wear a hat like that?—not only dared, but carry it off so magnificently. She heard Jordan Kerr give a derisive snort as Mrs Belmont, spotting Serena, held her hands out towards her in an affectionate welcome as she approached them.

'My congratulations,' he said softly. 'You've got her well trained, but I should imagine she's a little on the expensive side. I hope she's worth it!'

Moving forward to greet her mother, closely followed by Jordan, Serena did not bother to answer.

'Darling!' breathed Mrs Belmont as if it were six months since she had seen her instead of only one week.

As her mother kissed her cheek, Serena knew she was sizing up the man standing by her side. Nothing would go unnoticed, Serena knew. From his fine linen suit to his hand-made shoes, for Mrs Belmont was a snob—in the nicest possible way, of course. The only daughter of an impoverished Irish peer, she was used to moving in the right social circles and not unnaturally had high ambitions for Serena.

Having decided Jordan was 'acceptable', Mrs Belmont flashed him a brilliant smile and Serena was furious. Before she could speak Jordan said coldly, 'Shall we adjourn to a more private spot?' and placing a hand on Serena's arm shepherded them towards the airport lounge.

Mrs Belmont's eyebrows lifted slightly at this autocratic treatment and she glanced swiftly at Serena. Interpreting the look, Serena knew she was saying 'Well done', and it appeared her mother was labouring under the impression that Jordan Kerr was an impatient lover who intended to lose no time in making his intention clear to his beloved's only relation. She was, thought Serena grimly, in for a bit of a shock!

Reaching the lounge, he led them past the groups of people standing around and ushered them into a small office off the main ticket office.

As soon as the door was shut, Serena began hastily, 'Mother, would you ...'

'I'll do the talking,' cut in Jordan curtly. 'And you can drop the "Mother" stunt for a start.'

Had Serena not been so anxious to prove her identity the sight of her mother's bewildered face might have given her hysterics; as it was, she was tired of being bullied by this detestable man. 'No, you will not!' she replied furiously. 'You've had your say, Mr Kerr, now it's my turn. Mother,' she demanded, 'tell this man who I am!'

Mrs Belmont raised expressive eyebrows at this odd request. She was not, Serena noticed, a bit put out—almost, Serena thought crossly, as if this sort of question cropped up regularly!

'Who does Mr Kerr think you are?' Mrs Belmont inquired innocently.

Serena stared at her, not failing to note the grim expression on Jordan Kerr's face. 'For goodness' sake!' she exploded. 'This is serious, Mother!'

Jordan intervened swiftly with, 'It appears your friend catches on a bit quicker than you do,' adding silkily, 'When I tell her there isn't a hope of an inheritance perhaps she'll catch on even quicker.'

Serena had to hand it to her mother, she didn't bat an eyelid! 'Where's Roger?' she asked quickly, thinking if she didn't get some assistance in the very near future, she would scream the place down.

'That, darling, is the reason I've come,' replied her mother, keeping a wary eye on Jordan. 'The poor dear's had an accident. The driver of the other car was drunk, and Roger couldn't avoid hitting him. He's not seriously hurt, though, slight concussion and a suspected broken ankle. We've had to cancel the cruise, I'm afraid, for a week or two at least.' She cast another look at Jordan. 'We couldn't think what was keeping you. I've strict instructions to bring you back with me.'

'I regret that is out of the question,' cut in Jordan swiftly. 'I have no intention of releasing her.'

Mrs Belmont gave these words a little thought and Serena had a nasty feeling that she was well aware of Jordan Kerr's status, and in that respect he was certainly in the 'right' category as far as she was concerned! She made another desperate attempt to get through to her mother. 'When you've heard . . .'

'There's nothing to hear,' interjected Jordan, 'nothing she doesn't already know, or has guessed.'

His next words clinched the matter as far as Mrs Belmont was concerned. 'You can give Mr Alton my regards; you can also tell him Miss Belmont regrets she will be unable to join him on the cruise. She is going to be—er—rather tied up for the next few months.' He glanced at his watch and fixing a steely glance on Mrs Belmont, added haughtily, 'I suggest you take the next flight back. There's one in precisely ten minutes.'

Serena's mother blinked, then smiled knowingly at Serena. 'Your dear father was just the same,' she murmured mistily. 'He would brook no interference.' She smiled confidingly at Jordan. 'I'll forgive your obvious manoeuvre to get rid of me. You've nothing to worry about, you know, I'm quite harmless. However, I didn't intend to stay long anyway, someone's got to look after Roger. He's bound to fret until he knows Serena's all right.' She gave Serena a light kiss on the cheek. 'You will keep me informed, won't you, darling?'

Serena really didn't see the point of answering. No matter what she said it was bound to be misinterpreted, if not by her mother, then by Jordan Kerr, in any case she was saved the necessity.

'You need have no worries on that score,' Jordan assured her steadily as he opened the door to indicate the end of the discussion.

CHAPTER TEN

SERENA sat in a half dazed condition in Jordan Kerr's car as it glided smoothly out of the airport precincts. Bewilderedly she thought that if someone had told her of the position she would one day find herself in, she would have told them such things did not, could not, happen. People just did not behave like that— but they had! Her mother had for a start! She had gaily waved her farewell before boarding the plane back to New York.

For all she knew, Serena thought bitterly, she might have left her daughter to the tender mercies of a white-slaver. She sighed heavily; anyone else but the autocratic and wealthy Jordan Kerr would not have got away with it. The fact that her daughter had not only made the acquaintance of such an august personage, but apparently captivated him, had tipped the scales. Mrs Belmont, like Mrs Tonetti, was a firm believer in fate—in fact, they had quite a lot in common, Serena thought crossly; neither had proved exactly reliable in a crisis.

Gazing out at the waving palms that lined the road they were travelling down, Serena tried to cheer herself up with the thought that at least the worry of Roger suddenly descending on her had been effectively removed and she was now free to enjoy Mrs Tonetti's company—or at least she would be, if a certain character stayed out of her hair!

Serena was quite sure that if it had been anyone else but Jordan Kerr holding the whiphand she would have been more than willing to play the part allocated her; she was very fond of Mrs Tonetti and it would be no hardship seeing to her welfare. It was just that something about this man caught her on the raw. She didn't even mind his insults—he would be the one making the apologies later; no—it wasn't that. Serena frowned; in some ways he'd reminded her of Roger. Dominant was the word, she thought. Perhaps what she'd said to Mrs Tonetti that very morning was the truth? That her type of man was the meek and mild type? She gave an impatient shrug. Well anyway, it certainly wasn't the Jordan Kerr model!

'Worrying about the boy-friend's reaction?' Jordan asked smoothly. 'If so, I shouldn't. I've an idea your friend will think up some ploy to keep the pot boiling. Leave a bolthole open, as it were, in case things don't pan out this end. As I think I said, a very enterprising woman, that. I'm pretty sure she knew of me, not to mention what I'm worth.' He threw Serena a mocking look. 'Made no bones about leaving you, did she? Been in a similar situation, no doubt, and has every confidence of your coming home with the bacon again.'

'Do you mind if we drop the subject?' snapped Serena. 'You've got what you wanted. I stay and be a dutiful granddaughter. Just promise me one thing,' she ground out, 'to stay away from me from now on.'

'Come, Lisa,' he all but purred the words. 'We're almost engaged, aren't we?'

'You can drop that charade, too,' Serena replied furiously. 'It wouldn't be the first time you've suddenly lost interest, would it? I hear you're quite adept at it. My—er—grandmother thought it wise to drop me a hint on that score.' Her eyes flashed shoots of violet rays. 'Just say you've lost interest, I'll even play the part of the spurned woman to get you out of my vicinity. Say what you want—I don't care! Just leave me alone. It's not as if I can go anywhere, is it? You've got my passport,' she added bitterly.

He slowed the car down and pulled up in a layby and sat studying her for a moment or so with narrowed eyes. 'You seem to forget who's calling the tune,' he said in a dangerously soft voice. 'I like things as they are. That way I can keep an eye on you. No doubt it would suit your purpose if I drifted off the scene, but I'd never be certain, you see, that you hadn't hastened your grandmother's end.'

It took a moment or so for her to grasp the full implication of these words and when it did her eyes opened to their full capacity. 'You think I'd . . .' She couldn't go on.

His eyes registered the shock he had given her

and he shrugged casually. 'Oh, not consciously, perhaps,' he said curtly. 'But I wouldn't put it past you to vent your frustration out on her. No, Miss Tonetti, I'm not taking any chances. I'm going to be around for as long as it takes.' So saying, he started up the engine and steered the car back on to the road.

The rest of the journey was spent in silence, Serena was too shocked to attempt to break it. She was partially recovering when he threw the second bombshell. Arriving at the chalet, he accompanied the silent Serena to the lounge and before she could guess his intention said casually to Mrs Tonetti, 'I'm making Serena's stay permanent.'

There was no mistaking his meaning and Serena stood helplessly by his side trying to look deliriously happy, but she was absolutely stunned, and fortunately for her so was Mrs Tonetti. After a fractional pause she moved towards them, and with tear-dimmed eyes caught both of their hands in hers. 'Oh, my dears! I'm so happy for both of you,' she smiled.

Why doesn't she say I'm not Lisa? Serena thought frantically and tried to catch her eye, but Mrs Tonetti was too overcome to consider such mundane information suitable at this time.

Serena longed for Jordan to go so that she could get through to her the absolute necessity for the truth to come out, but her new-found fiancé had other plans. Giving her no respite, he pulled her up out of the chair she had thankfully sunk into, remarking cheerfully, 'We've got to get organised, darling. Come on!'

Sitting in Jordan's study a short while later, Serena watched dully as he twirled the knob of a heavy wall safe. 'This is one combination you'll not get,' he remarked caustically. 'The ring's insured too, but then you wouldn't be stupid enough to try and hang on to it, would you?'

Serena had not said a word since they had left Mrs Tonetti, but now, watching him remove a small leather box and carefully lock the safe after him, she whispered bitterly, 'Why?—why do you insist on going on with this farce?'

He had opened the box and stood looking at the contents. She saw his mouth twist slightly, and she thought she knew why; he was obviously thinking of the girl he had hoped would one day wear the ring. The small ornate box spoke of antiquity; the ring had probably been handed down through the centuries to prospective brides. Suddenly he glanced up at her, catching her unawares, and for a moment in time glinting green eyes pierced violet ones. Serena couldn't define that look, but it was as if they had gone back in time, not years, but centuries, and she felt the familiar tingling along her spine.

Whatever had affected her had touched him, too.

She was sure of it as she saw him mentally shake himself, and watched the familiar hardening of the jaw as he answered her earlier question.

'Because your grandmother is not a fool,' he said harshly. 'I'm afraid she knows me a little too well,' his glance was now mocking. 'As you so kindly pointed out when we left the airfield, I have been known to be somewhat fickle in my attentions to the fair sex.' His glance hardened. 'If she thought fit to warn you that could mean only one thing—she was worried about you. And that's not the only thing I suspect she had on her mind. She knows she's nothing to leave you, and it's my guess she's worrying about how she's going to tell you. Well, this little charade will set her mind at rest. Come here,' he ordered curtly.

Serena remained where she was. She guessed he wanted her to put the ring on and wondered why he didn't just throw the box at her. He certainly didn't intend to put himself out, she thought scathingly, and although what he'd said about Mrs Tonetti made sense, Serena was loth to commit herself to such a man, charade or no charade!

In three quick strides he was beside her and in no gentle fashion had grasped her left hand and held it up. Thrusting the ring into her right hand, he commanded, 'Put it on,' adding scathingly, 'I have no doubt it will have to be altered.'

Having no choice in the matter, Serena slipped

the ring on the third finger of her left hand, still held hard by Jordan.

It was a perfect fit; Serena was slightly surprised and a little disappointed as she had hoped fervently it wouldn't be.

Her surprise was nothing compared to Jordan's. His autocratic brows rose and he turned the hand towards him as if to certify the fact that the thick band of gold was not biting into the flesh of her finger. Then as if the contact stung him he withdrew his hold on her, leaving Serena staring at the imposing ring, its huge diamond centre piece flashing scintillating lights that screamed its value.

'I can't possibly wear it!' she exclaimed in a shocked voice. 'It must be worth a fortune!'

Jordan smiled cynically. 'It is,' he assured her grimly. 'Afraid you'll be tempted? Don't worry, before you've done your stint, you'll be glad to see the back of it. That ring,' he said silkily, 'gives me the right to seek you out at any time of my choosing.'

Serena's eyes spoke her thoughts, but she did not give way to anger; she had no wish to feel his iron hold on her again, so she took refuge in sarcasm. 'Surely you have some other little bauble that would do the job just as well?' She narrowed her eyes calculatingly as she held her hand up and studied the ring. 'You know, I could use this to bribe someone to get me off the island. Have you thought of that?' she queried innocently.

For a few seconds it looked as if he might well throttle her, but he mastered his emotions and shrugged casually. 'There isn't a soul on the island who would dare to cross me, Miss Tonetti. And,' his eyes were hooded as he added softly, 'I wouldn't advise you to try. You see, I might decide to save Alton from himself in spite of all the spade work your friend is putting in at her end, leaving the way clear for you to make a comeback. In your case, two birds in the bush is better than one in the hand, isn't it? Believe me, you accept my ultimatum or take the consequences. I can assure you Alton wouldn't touch you with a bargepole by the time I've finished with you. Nor would any self-respecting man!'

CHAPTER ELEVEN

Whatever reaction Serena might have given to Jordan Kerr's threats was never enacted, as a telephone call was received by him while she was busy gathering her forces for the onslaught.

His curt, 'We'll be right over,' told her he was in no mood for verbal battle, and his next words wiped out any inclination she had had to retaliate. 'Your grandmother,' he said tersely as he all but threw her light linen jacket she had left lying on a chair at her, and made for the door.

Serena barely had time to fling herself in the car seat before he took off. She wanted to ask what had happened, but something in Jordan Kerr's expression stopped her.

Within minutes they were sweeping up the drive to the chalet and, not waiting for Serena, Jordan was out of the car and into the chalet while Serena was still collecting her senses.

Although she had by now realised that whatever it was it was serious, she was still not prepared for what she heard the doctor tell Jordan as she came upon them in the hall. 'There's not much time, I'm afraid. She's asking for you and someone called Serena—her granddaughter, I believe.'

The doctor then caught sight of Serena standing hesitantly behind Jordan. 'Go in, my dear,' he said gently. 'It's a door we all have to pass through and she's quite ready to go. Don't be afraid.'

Serena was not afraid; the doctor had mistaken her hesitancy for fear. In fact, she did not feel anything; she was mentally and physically numb.

As she entered the cool shuttered room Mrs Tonetti lay in Molly raised tear-stained eyes towards her and put down the linen cloth she had just wrung out to place on Mrs Tonetti's forehead. She shook her head sadly as Serena's eyes met hers and mutely handed her the cloth, then softly left the room.

Gently wiping the perspiring face, Serena realised the old lady had sunk into a coma and was delirious. Suddenly her hand was caught. 'Lisa? Is that you?' Then came a subsided muttering and, 'Why did you leave? You didn't write. I was so worried.' The breathing quickened and again she asked, 'It is you, Lisa, isn't it? You've come back?'

Serena's eyes misted over; she patted the frail hand that moved restlessly across the linen sheet. 'Yes, it's Lisa, Nan,' she said softly. 'I'm here.'

A sigh of contentment followed this assurance and for a moment Mrs Tonetti clung to Serena's hand, then as if she hadn't the strength to keep it there it sank back on to the bed. Serena turned to the bowl of water on the side table to wring out the cloth once more and met the cynical eyes of Jordan Kerr standing just inside the door; something snapped inside her. His eyes were congratulating her on a fine performance. She looked back at Mrs Tonetti, who appeared to be sleeping peacefully, and unable to stand his presence, Serena walked past him out to the kitchen where Molly was hovering anxiously.

'I'm going to get some fresh air, Molly,' she said quietly. 'She's sleeping at the moment. I'll only be in the garden if she calls for me.'

The cool breeze from the bay fanned her face as she stood gazing out beyond the breakers clearly seen in the light of a brilliant tropical moon. The soft lapping of the waves as they met the shore lulled some sense of proportion into her, and she knew an infinite sadness. For a brief minute she hated Lisa Tonetti for what she had done to her grandparents. Where was she now? Serena wondered. Living it up as Jordan Kerr had intimated?

'It's a little late to be sorry for what you did, isn't it?' said the goading voice directly behind her. 'Or are you sorry? Or is it that you're missing the high life and wishing you were taking cocktails with another poor dupe?'

Serena would have liked to ignore him, but something spurred her on. 'What if I did feel compassion for her?' she said in a low voice that vibrated with pent-up tension. 'You wouldn't understand, anyway. Compassion is not an emotion you've ever felt. What if I were Lisa? Wouldn't I feel something? No one,' she said bitterly, 'is all bad, but you're so twisted inside you can't even entertain the thought that she might have stayed away because she was ashamed of what she had done.'

'And are you?' he said softly, then sighed elaborately. 'You know, I sometimes wish I had more faith in human nature, for you might have fooled me.'

A stifled sob behind them made them turn, to find Molly walking slowly towards them. Both were aware of the tidings she had to convey to them, although it was no less of a shock.

Jordan, laying a comforting arm around Molly's shoulders, escorted her back to the house, but Serena stayed where she was. A sob escaped her and the tears slid down her cheeks. She had never known her grandparents and she couldn't have been more fond of them than she had been of Mrs Tonetti.

'There's no need to overact the grieving relation bit,' Jordan's cold voice spoke behind her. 'The doctor's gone and Molly's lying down with a sedative.'

Serena turned towards him. He was so close she had only to lean forward and her head would rest on that strong shoulder so invitingly near. In her need for solace her bowed head rested wearily against him. 'Please, Jordan, not now,' she whispered.

For a brief second he stiffened, then with a soft

groan his arms crushed her to him and his lips found hers.

The kiss was savage, but it awoke an answering echo in Serena. It also awoke her to a world of beauty, of giving and taking, of desire and a certain knowledge that until this moment she had lived in a vacuum not really knowing what life was all about. She could even understand the brutality as her soft lips were ruthlessly pounded.

She knew that as she had sought consolation, so too did he. For one brief flight in time they met on another plane, each desperately needing one another.

Then she was flung from him and the fury in his voice brought her back to cold reality.

'So that's how it's done, is it?' he ground out. 'What am I supposed to do now—compensate you with a fat cheque? And be besotted enough to collect on the dividend? Well, it didn't come off. You couldn't even wait until after the funeral before trying your charms out on me, could you? Well, get this, and get it good. As far as I'm concerned you're a tramp—a high class one, maybe, but still a tramp. I'd sooner tangle with a scorpion! Now we've got that little business out of the way I suggest you go and pack. You've got thirty minutes in which to do it. I want you on that plane and off my land in the shortest possible time.'

Serena tried to collect her scattered wits. She was

being allowed to leave? Her start did not go unnoticed.

'Yes,' he jeered. 'Back to New York and your fancy friends, and they're more than welcome to you!'

'The funeral?' Serena asked hesitantly, thinking how odd it would look if she weren't there.

'Fancy yourself in black?' he inquired silkily. 'Or were you hoping there might still be a little something for you in the will? I'm sorry, but that's just not on. I want you off my land, pronto!'

He turned to go, then swung back to her. 'Haven't you forgotten something?' he asked in that hateful soft voice of his, and held his hand out. 'The ring, if you please.'

Serena gave another start. She had forgotten the ring, and with a quick movement she slipped it off her finger. She was about to hand it to him when he said, 'Did you hope I'd forgotten it? Or was that what the kiss was for?'

Goaded beyond all reason, Serena flung the ring at him. It landed at his feet, its brilliant stone picking up the rays from the moon lay flashing on the ground.

He made no move to retrieve it but looked at her. 'Pick it up,' he said in a dangerously soft voice.

In a voice that slightly trembled Serena replied, 'Pick it up yourself!'

Her arm was caught in that familiar iron hold and was forced down to where the ring lay. 'Now pick it up,' he said in a voice that brooked no argument.

This time he did leave, and Serena stood staring after him with the nails of her fingers digging into her palms.

CHAPTER TWELVE

SERENA's abrupt arrival in New York was met with surprise by her mother and barely concealed triumph by Roger, who adopted a 'you may kiss my hand' attitude, indicating to Serena that although she had hurt him he was quite willing to forgive her.

However, Serena was in no mood to respond to this kind of tactic; she was heartsick and incredibly weary; and the thought that her whole life had been turned upside down in such a short period of time seemed barely conceivable.

With a tact that Serena didn't know her mother possessed, she ushered her out of the room and into Serena's. Helping her unpack and ringing for a tray of tea, she chatted on about this and that, never once mentioning a certain person's name, although Serena knew she was consumed with curiosity. Come to that, so was Roger, but it was a curiosity that would have to remain unsatisfied until Serena was more in command of herself. She didn't want to think about it, but she knew she would; she also knew she ought to be thanking her lucky stars that it was all over.

No more worrying about saying the right thing or being treated as a second class citizen. No more Mrs

Tonetti; she hastily blinked away the mistiness this thought brought. She had to remember she had died happy; and she had been happy, Serena thought sadly, remembering her unconcealed delight at the news of the 'engagement'. Serena suspected it was this very event that had caused the collapse—too much excitement after years of loneliness.

She also suspected that Jordan Kerr had come to the same conclusion. It would, she thought wearily, account for that one weak moment when he had kissed her so savagely. Hastily she brought her thoughts back in an effort to try and concentrate on what her mother was talking about. Tomorrow, she told herself, she would see things in a different light, even be able to enjoy herself.

Serena hadn't even noticed that her mother had left the room until she came back and remarked happily, 'I've just left Roger organising the cruise. We leave as planned on Monday. He's sick and tired of being tied to the hotel room. Said he might as well collect a tan while he has to stay put until that ankle's stronger. He didn't break it, by the way.'

Giving her mother a wry smile for the tactful hint, Serena exclaimed, 'Oh dear, and I didn't even inquire how he felt!'

Mrs Belmont patted her daughter's hand. 'Well, you can make up for it during the cruise,' she said soothingly. 'I must say it's nice seeing him in good humour again.' She gave Serena a considering look.

'You know he's very fond of you, dear, don't you?'

Serena nodded dumbly, thinking Jordan Kerr hadn't been all that far off the mark where her mother was concerned. She wanted to see Serena happily married, but it had to be to a rich man, it would never occur to Mrs Belmont that the two might not go together. Poverty was a nasty word where she was concerned and happiness out of the question if the bank balance was slender.

On her own once more, Serena thought about the coming cruise and wished she could work up a little more enthusiam about it. Roger's excuse about getting a tan was a barely disguised ruse to keep her safe in close proximity. He was taking no chances of her doing the disappearing act again. Serena knew she ought to have been grateful that someone cared enough about her to adopt such strategy.

Two days later, while sunning herself on the deck of the luxury yacht, Serena came to a decision. If Roger asked her to marry him again, which she was certain would be any day now, she would agree.

Not because she loved him but because she had made the catastrophic discovery that she was hopelessly and irrevocably in love with Jordan Kerr. She did not try and delude herself that that love would ever be returned. He was as far out of her reach as he might have been had they never met; more so, she thought wearily, for he would never know the truth, and even if he did, he would only at the best feel apologetic, and in spite of her earlier thoughts on the matter Serena could not have borne that. She would far rather he went on hating her for what he thought she was.

She turned over on to her back and lay gazing up at the bright blue cloudless sky. Maria, she thought miserably. It all came back to Maria; how Jordan must have loved her! Serena's eyes moistened; whoever he eventually married would have to contend with a ghost. Would Myrna lay the ghost? Blinking the moisture away from her eyes, Serena couldn't believe that she would. She had only seen the hard side of his nature, but she was certain he was not a man to give his heart lightly. He would swear allegiance to but one woman, there would never be a second-best for him.

Mrs Tonetti had loved Maria too, and that, Serena thought, would endear Jordan to her. She felt a touch on her arm and glanced up to meet Roger's probing eyes.

'Ready to name the day?' he asked casually as he dropped down beside her.

Serena's voice was calm as she answered. He knows, she thought, he knows I'm in love with someone I can't have, but he doesn't care; he wants me enough to accept me on any terms. 'Ready when you are,' she replied just as casually.

Roger's breath caught and he pulled her up into

a sitting position to face him. Slowly his eyes went over her face and met her eyes. 'Finished careering off into the blue, have you?' he asked steadily.

Serena knew what he meant. He was asking if it was all over—or rather telling her it had better be, she thought wearily, and nodded mutely.

Satisfied, he drew her into his arms and held her possessively close to him. With his lips on her hair he murmured, 'You'll never regret it, darling.'

She had to steel herself to meet the kiss he gave her. His lips were firm and the kiss was not distasteful, but her whole being cried out against his touch. She tried hard to respond but failed miserably.

When Roger released her his eyes were narrowed and on her lips, then he said slowly, 'You'll have to do better than that, Serena. I've waited a long time for this moment. You gave your word and I don't intend to release you, so don't have any second thoughts, will you?' He got up stiffly and picked his stick up. Before he limped away, he said, 'I'm announcing the engagement at supper tonight; meanwhile, think about what I've just said.'

Serena couldn't help obeying these instructions; for one thing she was appalled by the change in Roger's attitude to her. Although she knew he was dominant and liked his own way, he had been very careful in the past to wield the velvet glove where she was concerned. By those few but devastating words she had been given an insight of the future that stretched before her as his wife.

He would not only be domineering, but a jealous and possessive husband. She swallowed. It was too late now to back out—not that he'd let her; he'd told her that, too.

The sound of laughter came from the bar in the cabin beneath where she was lying. Soon, she knew, her mother would come in search of her to congratulate her. Roger would, of course make a point of informing her first. The other members of the party that numbered a dozen, mostly business acquaintances of Roger's with either their wives or their girl-friends, would be advised of the event as Roger had intimated, at supper that evening.

He would probably arrange a fanfare of trumpets, she thought miserably; Roger was all for pomp and ceremony, and the ring he would slip on her finger in front of the gathered assembly? She narrowed her eyes. It would be ostentatious and very, very costly.

Thinking of one ring, another was invariably brought to mind and Serena could still feel the weight of it on her third finger even though it was no longer there. The tears pricked dangerously near the surface and making a vain effort to shake off these sad memories, she told herself with bitter humour that not every girl got engaged twice in one week and she really ought to feel honoured!

Mrs Belmont, when she had managed to tear herself away from a Mr Janson, a widower and rich industrialist, who had formed a predilection for her company, finally located her daughter in her cabin preparing to dress for the supper party.

'Darling!' she exclaimed, pulling Serena close, 'I'm so happy for you. I knew you would say yes eventually, but I was so afraid you ...' she hesitated as she met Serena's eyes. 'Well,' she went on lamely, 'money isn't everything, is it?'

Serena started to laugh, but she wasn't really laughing, it was more in the nature of a mild attack of hysterics. Of all the people to make such a profound statement ... !

'Serena?' asked Mrs Belmont uncertainly, not liking the lost, haunted look in her daughter's eyes.

Wiping her eyes, Serena smiled wanly. 'It's all right, Mother. I suppose the past events have caught up with me. I know it's for the best, and I suppose one day I'll ...' she choked on the last few words, then pulled herself together. 'You'd better get ready, hadn't you? And I must hurry or Roger will be pounding on the door demanding to know what's keeping me.'

Mrs Belmont had never known her daughter to be unhappy, and she loved her very much. For the first time she realised, somewhat belatedly, that what she had been urging Serena to do for months might not bring her the happiness she so desperately wanted for her. 'Darling, you don't have to ... Roger will ...' she began hesitantly.

Giving her a wry smile, Serena pushed her to the door. 'I said it's going to be all right,' she said firmly. 'Stop worrying and let me get on and dress.'

Mrs Belmont did leave then, but it was obvious she had a lot on her mind, and Serena, wearily closing the cabin door after her, knew she wouldn't leave it at that. As for what she had said about Roger understanding, or would have said if given the opportunity, Serena sighed; her mother didn't know Roger half as well as she thought she did, and if she made any attempt to talk him out of the engagement she was in for a rude awakening.

Serena wore the white organdie gown she had worn at Jordan's ball. It brought back painful memories, but so would her blue velvet, she thought miserably. She couldn't discard them, they were the only evening dresses she had brought with her. A tap on the cabin door told her Roger was waiting for her and the look he gave her brought his last words sharply into focus again, and Serena almost shivered as he silently pulled her into his arms before escorting her to supper.

His kiss was fierce and demanding and again she tried to respond, and once again failed. The little smile he gave at her quick withdrawal from his arms worried Serena even more than his words had done. It promised firm action later that evening when they were alone.

She knew a moment's panic, then firmly took herself in hand. She was only getting engaged, after all, not married. She could still break it off if Roger persisted in treating her as if he owned her body and soul.

The small but luxurious dining room was as yet half empty when they arrived, and two stewards stood by waiting to serve the meal. The others would be taking their aperitifs in the bar and Serena, knowing Roger would wait until they were all seated before making the announcement, fervently hoped they would take their time.

She wondered if she were dreaming when the cry went up. 'Pirates!' shrieked a feminine voice. Then there were more shrieks and then laughter. Serena glanced at Roger, but he was as nonplussed as she. His eyebrows rose a fraction, then one of the guests, meeting his eyes, grinned. 'It's a stunt, I expect. We're not far from Blue Island, I believe it's one of the attractions there.'

Blue Island! The very name started Serena's heart palpitating. What if Jordan were one of them? Her mouth felt dry. She prayed that if he were present he would stay on deck and having made an appearance, make his departure with equal speed! Only too well could she imagine his reaction on seeing her on board, and with Roger! As usual, his eyes would say it all.

Suddenly the laughter and shrieks grew louder, and the next moment the room seemed filled with 'pirates'.

Against her will Serena's eyes were drawn to their leader, standing so straight and tall in front of his men. Almost as if he knew I was here, she thought bewilderedly as his eyes met hers and stayed on hers as he walked slowly towards their table.

Feeling a distinct urge to run, Serena gripped her serviette tightly and tried to break that mesmeric hold he had on her.

Reaching their table, Jordan gave them a mocking bow and Roger, entering into the spirit of the thing, said, 'I'm afraid we've no treasure on board, old man, but you're welcome to as much rum as you can sink.'

Jordan's eyes slowly left Serena and turned to Roger. 'Oh, but you have treasure,' he murmured softly, his eyes returning to Serena. 'And I'm afraid I'm going to relieve you of it.'

Even if she had wanted to move, Serena couldn't. It was as if her limbs were turned to jelly. He's playing with me again, she told herself wildly. She couldn't go through that again, anything was better than that. 'Roger——' she began desperately, but the rest of the sentence was never uttered as she found herself firmly caught and slung into a vaguely familiar position over Jordan's broad shoulders.

In sheer panic she struggled to release herself, but she knew from past experience that she was not going to be successful.

The action had so surprised Roger it had taken a

second or so for him to recover and he made an attempt to free the struggling Serena, but he was handicapped by his ankle. 'I think the joke's gone a little too far,' he commented caustically. 'Would you mind releasing my fiancée?'

Jordan's grasp on Serena tightened as he looked back at Roger. 'I saw no ring,' he commented casually. 'Besides, she makes a habit of getting engaged, didn't you know? I intend to cure that tendency!' he added as he turned towards the door with his unwilling captive.

Roger made a grab at his stick and glared at the grinning men around him. 'John!' he commanded to one nearest him. 'For heaven's sake, do something! Don't just stand there grinning!'

'It's okay, old man,' replied John, 'I've seen it all before. He'll return her within a short while.'

Jordan stopped in his tracks and turned back to the company. 'I regret I must disabuse you. This is one prize I shall not be returning.' This assertion, though quietly said, set up shock waves.

Serena, still struggling, saw a general surge forward in a late effort to rescue her, but Jordan's men formed a line between them and the door.

The last person Serena saw before she was so unceremoniously bundled out of the dining room was her mother, and she was certain she had given her a wicked wink!

CHAPTER THIRTEEN

JORDAN did not release her until he had watched the rearguard of his men leave the yacht and join what looked like a small flotilla of motor boats stationed alongside. Then his deep voice gave the order, 'Let's away, Jake!' and the air was filled with the deep throbbing of the engines and one by one the small fleet swept out to sea.

Serena felt herself lowered to the deck of the powerful motor boat now making fast headway in the lead of the other boats, and she watched the twinkling lights of the yacht dwindle into dimness as the distance between the boat and the yacht was lengthened.

She was only too aware of Jordan standing close beside her, ready if need be to lay a restraining hand on her should she try to make a break for the side. Tensely she wondered what nasty little surprise he had up his sleeve for her this time. He must have decided she had got off a little too lightly and thought up some other way she could pay her debt to society.

When his voice spoke close to her ear she started and moved slightly away from him. 'Shall we go below?' he suggested.

The heavy throb of the boat's engines made normal conversation impossible, but whatever he had to say Serena preferred to hear it right there and then; the breeze playing over her face and the spray sending up white plumes of water that sprayed over the deck would, she felt, help lessen the shock. 'I'm quite happy where I am,' she replied, trying to sound casual.

His reply was to sweep her off her feet and carry her down the two shallow steps leading to the cabin. 'As I believe I told you once before,' he remarked airily, 'Milady has no choice in the matter.'

As if she had no power left in her legs he put her down gently on one of the leather-covered chairs in the small salon, then sat down opposite her.

Serena watched him warily as he slipped the bandanna off his head and solemnly laid it on her lap. Without taking his eyes off her he said slowly and very distinctly, 'Marry me, Serena Belmont.'

A slightly stunned Serena realised he was telling her he now knew who she was. Her dazed eyes left his and rested on the bandanna.

'It's a custom of ours,' he said gently. 'Another way of laying our heart at the feet of the woman of our choice.'

Hardly recognising her own voice, Serena whispered huskily, 'Why?'

'Why the custom—or why the proposal?' he replied lightly. 'I'll tell you about the custom some

166

other time. As for the proposal—well, there's only one reason a man asks a woman to marry him, and I'm no exception to the rule.'

He got up suddenly and pulled her into his arms. 'We're wasting time,' he said in a voice even deeper that its normal tone as he drew her closer into the circle of his arms.

With all her heart Serena wanted to respond; the love she had thought was denied her was hers for the taking. Why then did she hesitate? What perverse streak of nature held her back? Afraid to meet his eyes, she concentrated on his broad chest and noted absently how a thread of her dress had got entangled in the fine stitching of his jerkin. Then she had it: Maria! Maria was, had been, his woman; there would be no other. The thing she had been so afraid would happen had happened. He was now sorry for her—that kiss, she thought bitterly, remembering how she had melted in his arms and the shameless way she had clung to his lips. He knew she loved him! There could be no other answer for his gallant but heartbreaking offer.

Somehow she summoned up the strength to release herself from his hold and rushed to the door. She needed to get as far as possible from him; she didn't trust herself not to break down and be coerced into accepting his offer and spending the rest of her life competing with Maria's ghost.

Her hand was on the door when he reached out

one long arm and hauled her back again. This time there was no escape from those strong arms of his. He caught the back of her head and made her look up at him.

'Leave me alone,' she whispered pleadingly.

'I'll never leave you alone,' Jordan answered harshly. 'And you might as well accept that fact. I meant every word I said back there. I've got you and I'll keep you. You've got a lot to atone for. From the day you agreed to become Mrs Tonetti's accomplice you turned my well-ordered existence into a living hell. Can you,' he said in a dangerously soft voice, 'imagine my feelings when the one and only woman I could ever care for descends on me in the guise of the woman who had caused so much unhappiness to two very dear friends of mine? And there you stood looking like a Raphael painting. I loved you the moment I set eyes on you and spent the rest of that hellish time trying to hate you.'

He pulled her fiercely closer and sought her lips saying as his met hers, 'Don't try and deny me, my love. I won't be denied.'

There was still Maria, she thought miserably as his lips at last released hers. Even now, as weak as she was in his arms, she couldn't forget Maria.

Holding her away from him, Jordan saw the hesitation in her eyes and mistaking it for uncertainty of her feelings for him, said softly, 'I remember someone turning to me for comfort. I also remember lips wanting mine as much as I wanted them.'

Serena could have wept, instead she gathered her forces for her last defence. His words had given her the spur she so badly needed. Her lovely eyes met his levelly as she said, 'And Maria?'

Her heart leapt painfully as she watched his start at the name. That was one little fact he hadn't accounted for, she thought bitterly, and one that made a nonsense of his declaration that she was the only woman he had ever cared for. Serena thanked providence that she had kept her head and had not given way to her feelings. Now he would have to take those words back and the bald truth would at last come out.

She shivered; she didn't want to hear them, it was enough that she had been saved the painful knowledge before she accepted his proposal. She jerked herself away from him and walked over to the porthole and stood gazing out vaguely wondering where they were and whether he would take her back to Roger afterwards.

'How did you know about Maria?' he began.

Serena cut in wearily, 'Does it matter? I know, that's all. And I'd be grateful if you would return me to the yacht.'

She shivered again as she felt his arms slide round her waist and pull her close to his hard body. 'We'll forget that last request, if you don't mind,' he said firmly. 'Now about Maria,' he went on as he forced the struggling Serena to subside her efforts to release herself. 'Whether you like it or not, you're going to hear. There's going to be no skeletons in this family cupboard.' Then musingly he added, 'Mrs Tonetti, of course—I ought to have known!'

He turned the now weak Serena round to face him and because she had no strength was able to coax her to lay her head against his shoulder. 'That's better,' he said gently. 'Now let me tell you about Maria, who was beautiful and very spoilt. She was also born with the unfortunate knack of wanting what she couldn't have.' He paused for a second or so as his lips touched Serena's hair. 'As she grew older she had many admirers, but I'm afraid I was not among them. It might have been better if I had been. You see, I presented a challenge to her. At first it was slightly amusing; she would try little tricks to gain my attention; later, however, it became a down-right embarrassment. It didn't help when my father encouraged her. He wanted to see me settled and thought Maria would make the ideal wife for me. He was of course slightly biased because of the long-standing friendship between our two families.

'After my father died I was able to avoid the get-togethers that occurred every weekend. Because of business connections I had to do a lot of travelling and that way was able to partially sever old com-mitments. However, I'm afraid Maria was a very determined girl and whether I was on the island or

away on business, she would still spend her weekends here.'

Serena stirred in his arms. She had heard enough,
now she was able to understand. Jordan's eyes met
hers and the love she saw in them made her catch her
breath. Then he pulled himself together sharply
and went on. 'That's how she became acquainted
with Mrs Tonetti,' he said quietly. 'She used to stay
with her when they came over on holiday.'

There was another pause and Senera sensed he
was coming to the part he most disliked, but she
knew he would not be put off from relating it. 'I
was here the weekend she died,' he said slowly. 'One
of her manoeuvres to get my attention backfired
with the tragic result of her death. It wasn't the first
time she would do something crazy and land herself
up in a position from which she had to be rescued,
always of course with the knowledge that I was in
the near vicinity, for that was the sole object of the
exercise, and in spite of repeated warnings that the
next time I'd leave her to get herself out of trouble,
she still persevered.' His voice deepened and Serena
wound her arms round his neck. She could guess
what came next.

'Not that I ever would have done,' he said wearily.
'It was just that I wasn't where she thought I was.
There's a special spot on the southern point of the
island where I used to go fishing. It's pretty inacces-
sible unless you know the way, and for my own peace

and solitude I made pretty certain it stayed that way. Jake is the only other one who knows. Well, Maria couldn't get that information, but she did know approximately where my line would reach the water, and although she knew full well the dangers of swimming in that area it didn't deter her. She was a pretty strong swimmer anyway.

'I don't know what actually happened, but my guess is she called for help—which I might add she had done on several other occasions when she wasn't in the slightest danger. No matter, had I been there no doubt I would have gone in to rescue her. That's the trouble with a joker, you can never tell whether it's the real thing, or not. Having acted as though she were in trouble, I believe she found she had underestimated her own strength to battle with the elements.'

For a while he was silent and Serena hoped he had finished, but there was more.

'Afterwards, I found out that she had deliberately misconstrued our relationship. Goodness knows what she had told Mrs Tonetti, but it was a plain fact that the whole island had been waiting for our engagement to be announced. To contradict the fabrication after her death would have looked callous—besides, it served no purpose.'

His arms tightened around Serena. 'So you see, my love, why I kept a healthy distance from any other designing female. I learnt a hard lesson and one that kept me safe until I met my destiny.'

After his lips had hungrily reached once more for hers, he said huskily, 'After I kissed you that night I knew my feelings were too strong and that I'd never be able to keep you at arm's distance. I also knew, or thought I knew, how quickly you'd catch on to that fact and would capitalise on it. As much as I hated you for what I thought you were, I wanted you so badly I would have been lost in the end. I had to send you away from me. When you'd gone I wandered back to Mrs Tonetti's. It was as if I couldn't keep away. I wanted to see the room you'd slept in, to touch the pillow that your head had lain against. I think I was half crazy.' He drew a deep breath. 'Then Molly gave me a letter, a letter that brought a rainbow into the room and that made me want to shout for joy. I was impatient to claim my one and only love, and the thought that I'd sent you back to the arms of Alton was almost unbearable.' He ran his hands through her long silky hair. 'But I couldn't leave right then. There were things to be seen to.'

Serena knew he was referring to Mrs Tonetti's death. 'Jordan, did we ...'

He understood the question. 'I don't know, my love. Perhaps; but one day I'll let you read the letter she left for me. One thing I can tell you, my darling, she died happy.' There was another pause, then he said softly, 'You know, I think it would be rather nice if we named our second child after her.'

Serena's heart turned over and meeting his eyes she stammered, 'Second child?'

He nodded autocratically. 'Of course; the Kerr's first-born is always a boy, and you won't need three guesses to know his christian name!'

So saying, he swept her back into his arms. 'You're too far away,' he complained.

YOU'LL L♥VE
Harlequin Magazine

for women who enjoy reading fascinating stories of exciting romance in exotic places

SUBSCRIBE NOW!

This is a colorful magazine especially designed and published for the readers of Harlequin novels.

Now you can receive your very own copy delivered right to your home every month throughout the year for only 75¢ an issue.

This colorful magazine is available only through Harlequin Reader Service, so enter your subscription now!

In every issue...

Here's what you'll find:

♥ a complete, full-length romantic novel...illustrated in color.

♥ exotic travel feature...an adventurous visit to a romantic faraway corner of the world.

♥ delightful recipes from around the world...to bring delectable new ideas to your table.

♥ reader's page...your chance to exchange news and views with other Harlequin readers.

♥ other features on a wide variety of interesting subjects.

Start enjoying your own copies of Harlequin magazine immediately by completing the subscription reservation form.

Not sold in stores!